A Candlelight Ecstasy Romance®

"I DON'T WANT TO HEAR ABOUT YOUR PREVIOUS LOVE LIFE," SHE PROTESTED.

Hearing the name of the woman he must have loved to distraction hurt as much as his rejection of her own less-than-perfect body. "I'm not going to listen."

"You will listen. You will hear. And you will understand why I stopped making love to you."

Her lips clamped tight; she began humming loudly.

"Stop it, Sara! I didn't carry you down here with some perverted idea of making you want me, then refusing at the last minute."

The tuneless hum droned louder. He couldn't make her listen if she didn't want to.

"I can shout louder than you can hum," Ryan yelled. "Susan jilted me!"

CANDLELIGHT ECSTASY ROMANCES®

A WHOLE LOT OF WOMAN

Anna Hudson

A CANDLELIGHT ECSTASY ROMANCE®

Published by
Dell Publishing Co., Inc.
1 Dag Hammarskjold Plaza
New York, New York 10017

ISBN: 0-440-19524-1

Printed in the United States of America

First printing—June 1985

To Our Readers:

We have been delighted with your enthusiastic response to Candlelight Ecstasy Romances®, and we thank you for the interest you have shown in this exciting series.

In the upcoming months we will continue to present the distinctive sensuous love stories you have come to expect only from Ecstasy. We look forward to bringing you many more books from your favorite authors and also the very finest work from new authors of contemporary romantic fiction.

As always, we are striving to present the unique, absorbing love stories that you enjoy most—books that are more than ordinary romance. Your suggestions and comments are always welcome. Please write to us at the address below.

Sincerely,

The Editors
Candlelight Romances
1 Dag Hammarskjold Plaza
New York, New York 10017

CHAPTER ONE

"Is that a paper clip I see you using to bundle those ten-dollar bills?" Ryan Crosby asked in a suitably hushed tone for an officer at the People's Bank.

Inwardly Sara Hawkins groaned; outwardly she eased off the high banker's stool to her feet. *Mr. No-Sense-of-Humor Crosby is on patrol,* she silently grumbled, knowing she was about to receive another "your cash drawer is a pigsty" lecture. The man was an authority on pigsties. Must have been brought up in one, she thought grumpily.

"And what, pray tell, is this?" he asked, pointing to the contents of her cash drawer.

Sara raised her blue eyes from his tie tack, past his starched white collar, to his grim straight-lined lips, on to his scorn-filled brown eyes. "Fingernail polish," she replied, forgetting the required "sir."

"And this?"

"A pretzel." As the tip of his dark eyebrow

winged toward the razor-sharp part in his hair, she tacked on "sir."

He held the pretzel between his forefinger and thumb as though he had found the original serpent in the world's most widely read book. The scissors Sara had been using to clip a mouth-size piece off the pretzel were clamped shut. The silence between them was deafening, until Crosby began a tirade on neatness.

She didn't have to listen to his spiel. She knew it by heart. *You're the head teller. You're supposed to set an example. How would you feel if Richard Grant stored his aftershave in his money drawer? Or Marge Cransan's spare set of false teeth were prominently displayed in her cash drawer? Inexcusable, Miss Hawkins. Utterly inexcusable.*

The people and the items varied with each speech, but the intent remained the same: *Clean up your act!*

Sara had heard the lecture one time too often. Didn't the dark-haired giant towering over her realize when he bellied up to her, all she could see was the inside of his nose? *Sort of like standing at the foot of Mount Rushmore,* she thought, stifling a giggle. The scissor snipped again.

"How many times have I talked to you about the contents of your drawers?"

"Let me think. Two weeks ago you ate the Oreo cookie I had stashed away. Last month you snitched the Snickers, and on Valentine's Day you . . ."

Her lips curved up spontaneously, but she no-

12

ticed his were grimly clamped together. He couldn't take lighthearted teasing. The pulse at his throat throbbed with pent-up anger.

"Your 'pleasantly plump' body would starve if you weren't allowed to munch the day away," he commented, letting the pretzel plunk back among the one-dollar bills.

"Are you calling me fat?" Sara snarled, the smile fading. Constructive criticism was one thing, but criticizing her construction was another. "I'm not fat; I'm . . . fluffy."

Snorting ungraciously, Ryan Crosby let his pebble-hard eyes slide over her rounded curves. His mannerly attempts to get Sara to keep the food out of her cash drawer repeatedly failed. Perhaps he could encourage tidiness by referring to her ample build. How could a conscientious employee, dedicated to her work the way Sara was, put her hand into such a rat's nest? Her position demanded neatness, orderliness, Ryan thought, restraining from repeating the same reprimand he had given her on numerous previous occasions.

Sara pointed the tip of the scissors at his jugular vein. *One quick stab, and he'd think fluff instead of fat,* she told herself. *Where does bag-of-bones get off calling me fat?*

"You must have had a hot dog for lunch. There's mustard on your tie," she whispered, a wicked, impulsive gleam lighting her bright blue eyes. *You want neat,* she thought. *I'll give you a lesson in neat.*

Ryan automatically looked down just in time

13

to see Sara grab the tail end, raise her scissors, slide them beneath his Windsor knot, and . . . clip, clip. Severed from the knot, five inches of expensive silk fabric fell over the tie tack.

"There, now it's gone," Sara whispered conspiratorially as she twirled back to the front of the bank and nonchalantly began waiting on the customer who had witnessed her perfidy.

Serendipity Sara strikes again, she thought, mentally cursing her impetuous nature. Ears perked, she listened for a mighty roar from behind her. Regardless of the provocation, Mr. Humbug Crosby wasn't going to tolerate having his immaculate presence destroyed by an employee. Shifting her weight nervously from foot to foot, she waited for the ax to fall.

Her fingers struck three keys on the teller's machine as she tried to enter the customer's deposit. Instead of a hundred-dollar deposit, she had recorded a million-dollar deposit. Flustered, knowing by the blond hair raised on the back of her neck that Crosby was still behind her, she began correcting her second error of the day with a ball-point pen.

I was looking for a job when I came here eight years ago, she philosophized, rolling her eyes at the customer when the ink solidly refused to flow out of the point of the pen. *And it appears as though I'll be looking for another job . . . soon!* The male depositor didn't notice Sara's apprehension. His eyes were glued to the red stain emerging from beneath the collar of the bank's vice-president and flooding over his darkly tanned face.

"Here you are, Mr. Balkins. Have a good day, and I'll see you next Friday," Sara said, covering her anxiety by smiling sweetly as she handed the customer his receipt. "Mr. Balkins?" Sara followed the direction of the customer's bugged eyes and saw her boss ripping the remains of his tie from beneath his collar as he purposefully strode toward his glass-enclosed office.

"You gonna be here next week?" Mr. Balkins asked, taking the deposit receipt and slipping it into his billfold.

Sara leaned forward and whispered, "You wouldn't want the VP to walk around the bank with lunch all over his tie without knowing it, would you? I did him a favor."

Mr. Balkins grinned. "Something tells me he didn't appreciate your method of removing stains. Why don't you slip me a few samples and we'll run away to South America?" he said jokingly.

"Why, Mr. Balkins, shame on you. Next you'll be sliding a note over the counter that says, 'Give me all you've got.' "

Laughing as he shook his head, he quipped, "According to Mr. Crosby, you couldn't fit into a brown paper sack, could you?"

Sara raised her arm, muscleman fashion, and flexed it. "All muscle, Mr. Balkins. Mine is a little bit more relaxed than everyone else's."

"You're lovable, relaxed muscle and all," he gallantly replied. "See you next Friday."

She grinned at the weekly customer's back as he walked toward the front door. *You're lovable* echoed in her ears. She wondered if the unemployment service would find her lovable.

Mentally she reviewed her options. Typically short on forethought, Sara often tried to reconstruct impetuous moments in an effort to reach saner conclusions. She could have slapped Crosby's face. Too trite. A smile curved her lips. Punching him in the mouth and giving him a fat lip would have been satisfying. *No, no, Sara,* she thought self-chidingly. *He probably hits back.* She rubbed her index finger over the cupid's-bow curve of her lower lip. When she got off the chair, she could have scrunched his big toe with the weight of her "pleasantly plump" body. Sara shook her head, abruptly making her short blond curls bounce into complete disorder. No, he hadn't called her fat until after the neatness lecture.

She hadn't worried about her weight in years, and all of a sudden her boss's referring to it had made her angry enough to give him a tie adjustment with her scissors. Why had she let Ryan Crosby's snide remark bother her? Size wasn't her problem. How other people perceived her didn't affect her own self-worth. Hadn't she rationally decided during college she wasn't overweight but undertall? She was the perfect weight for someone seven feet tall. Besides, if God had meant her to be thin, he would have given her fewer fat cells. She couldn't help it if skinny people burned calories in their sleep while she hoarded them.

How could she be expected to maintain her weight without nibbling a little bit here and there during the day? she mused, hungrily glancing at the soft pretzel Crosby had dropped. After all, being plump required diligent calorie counting. One didn't gain curves overnight or keep them by daintily nibbling on rabbit food.

"Born two hundred years too late in the wrong country," Sara muttered.

Rubens, the artist, would have raved over her dimples. No bony, knockkneed lady was Sara Hawkins. When a man saw her from front or back, he knew he'd seen a whole lot of woman. Crabby Crosby simply didn't have an artistic eye. His problem, not hers.

Joining the ranks of the unemployed—now that's another matter, she thought as she scissored off a hunk of pretzel and furtively popped it into her mouth. The granular pieces of salt exploded on her taste buds, giving her instantaneous oral gratification. The chewy texture of the dough appeased her need to grind her back molars. Eight years of diligence down the tubes with a snip of the scissors.

Sara hooked her spiked heels through the bar on the rung of the stool, balanced herself on the steel covering of the burglar alarm, and raised herself to peek over the top edge of the Formica countertop. Ryan had removed the two-inch tie and replaced it with another. *Must have been a*

Boy Scout, she thought with impish glee. *Always prepared.*

His color was back to normal, she noted, watching him open the storage cabinet and extract a bundle of money straps. He tossed them onto his desktop hard enough for them to bounce a couple of times. Then he yanked a piece of typing paper from his side drawer and sat down.

A customer approaching her window distracted Sara from further spying.

"Hi, Sara. How's tricks?" The owner of the local dog obedience school grinned as he asked his standard question.

"Great. Last week I embezzled more than I earned," she said lightly. "Shall I deduct ten percent of your deposit now or cleverly manipulate the books later?"

"Small deposit. You'd better let me take you out to lunch instead," he replied, lowering one eyelid seductively. "Black-Eyed Pea has a special on Texas fried steaks with home-style gravy."

"You're tempting me," Sara answered, chuckling.

Over the years she and most of the regular depositors had developed a rapport other employees of the bank envied. Sara liked people, and in return they liked her. The missing filter between her brain and her mouth allowed her to say outrageous things that amused the customers and made them laugh.

"Three choices of vegetables, hot rolls, blackberry cobbler," he said to tempt her further, and he licked his lips.

Sara closed her eyes and envisioned the delicious food. "You sure know how to get to a woman's heart," she murmured. "But I've taken my lunch break."

"How about one day next week?"

"Same special?"

"Yep." He reached over and patted her hand affectionately. "Think I could train you to kiss me all over my face the way the puppies do?"

Handing him his receipt, she whispered in a hushed voice, "You want your face washed? You're propositioning the wrong girl. The only thing I'm interested in licking is an ice cream cone."

"Okay, okay," he responded, laughing and raising his hands. "Blue Bell Ice Cream Parlor after lunch."

A moonbeam grin rounded her face. "Keep talking about food, and I'm liable to perish before your eyes. Next Wednesday sound okay?"

"Wednesday it is. You don't mind if the kids join us, do you?"

"What about Mary?"

"She's dieting. Wouldn't be caught within ten blocks of a mashed potato," he answered. Surreptitiously he cupped his mouth with one hand. "I think she sneaks dog biscuits on the sly."

Sara laughed at the ridiculous suspicion. "Much as I'm tempted, you know my policy: Don't go out with married men unless their wives are along," she said, declining a lunch that made her stomach growl in rebellion against her self-imposed policy. Turning down a free meal should be at the bottom of her list of priorities.

"I'll ask again when Mary is below a hundred pounds and stuffing herself again."

"You do that." Sara smiled and placed the deposit in the proof operator's basket. "Have a scrumptious lunch, and think of me, slaving away, starving, trying to earn a pittance of a living."

"Next week I'll have plenty of money in the bank. Feel free to embezzle fifteen or twenty percent," he said and waved as he laughed and left the bank.

"Sara," the teller in the next cage whispered, "won't you get into trouble if Mr. Crosby hears you joking about . . ." The blasphemous word seemed to be lodged behind Richard Grant's tobacco-stained teeth.

"Embezzling?" The concern she heard laced in Grant's question touched Sara. Grant, a confirmed middle-aged bachelor, somewhat persnickety, with the cleanest cash drawer in the bank, didn't intimidate Sara. His timidity was the perfect foil for her own precociousness. "Don't worry, Richard. I'm stealthily covering my tracks."

"Oh, Sara," he moaned, his brow furrowing, his wire frame glasses sliding to the end of his nose, "You're in big trouble with Mr. Crosby as it is. I think he'd like to see you strung up by the thumbs for cutting his tie. He's particular about his appearance, you know."

"You think giving him a bow tie is worse than stealing money from the bank?" Sara said jokingly.

Richard turned bright red and began stammering, "N-n-n-no! B-b-b-ut . . ."

Sara laughed in a kindly manner. "Don't worry, Richard. I promise not to wear my diamonds and furs obtained through nefarious means to the scene of the crime." Because his face still looked as though asphyxiation were imminent, Sara reassured Richard by saying, "You're safe. Old bonehead wouldn't recognize an embezzler if he saw him take the money out of the till and shove it in his pocket . . . or purse, as the case may be."

"Shhhhhhhhh." Richard shushed her, placing one finger over his lips and glancing nervously about the lobby. "There are some things you can't fool around about. You're too nice a girl to end up in a federal prison."

"Yeah," Sara said, her eyes twinkling. "The food is supposed to be substandard."

Giving up hope of reforming Sara, Richard sighed heavily and began counting and strapping the extra money in his cash drawer. *Crosby should give him a trophy for making certain that the two parallel lines of the band are folded precisely at the edge of the stack of money and that the amount of the denomination rests squarely over the President's picture*, Sara thought, smiling. When he licked the glue on the back of the money strap, he probably premeasured it in his mouth to make certain there wasn't too much or too little. Richard carefully stamped the strapped cash with his Teller No. 5 stamp. Sara could almost hear the sigh of satisfaction humming through his lips.

"Sara, Mr. Crosby asked me to deliver these." Nancy Colston, Crosby's secretary, extended a small stack of money wrappers of various denominations and a sealed envelope with Sara's name boldly scrawled across the front.

"Gosh! A Christmas bonus in June. Isn't he the sweetest boss you've ever had?" Sara asked with exaggerated enthusiasm.

"Crosby?" Nancy squawked. "If you think he's sweet, I think you had better visit the local shrink. You've finally crossed the line between genius and insanity. He has to be the meanest, orneryest—"

"Tsk-tsk-tsk, Nancy Colston. Christmas is coming, and you won't get your bonus if you bad-mouth the boss."

"I'll get the same thing I did for Secretary Day: a disposable lighter." Nancy grinned. "Do you think one of these days he'll notice I quit smoking?"

Sara slit the end of the envelope open, blew a puff of air into the end, then pulled out a thin sheet of bank stationery. Silently she read the message: "I'll be at your condo at seven o'clock to pick up the new tie you're going to buy immediately after work. Crosby."

"Are you fired?" Richard whispered anxiously, his eyes barely peering over the edge of the teller's cage.

"Not yet," Sara replied with obvious relief. A cheeky grin tilted her lips sky-high. "It's a love letter. Crosby is hot for my bod."

Richard made a strangled sound. Nancy boisterously laughed aloud.

"You have to have a heart to fall in love," Nancy quipped. "Crosby had his removed for operating inefficiently."

"Shhhhhhh," Richard said. "What if he hears you two? We'll all be fired."

"Stop worrying. I tell you the man is crazy about me. Didn't you notice he could hardly keep his hands to himself earlier?" Sara could feel the wind whistling through her ears. Her fertile imagination was being fed by the desire to extinguish any concern about a rift between herself and the boss.

Opening the stationery again, she pretended to read: "Dearest Snookums." She placed her hand over the collar of her pink silk blouse and whispered, "A little pet name he likes to call me when we're alone." She cleared her throat dramatically, then continued reading. "Can hardly wait to wrap my arms around your luscious body. See you tonight at the love nest. Poopsy."

Nancy grabbed for the letter. "Snookums? Poopsy?"

"Wait," Sara said, slapping at her grabby fingers. "There's a postscript. Blow me a kiss if you'll be there."

"Now I know you're lying. He'd consider a

kiss worse than an obscene gesture." Nancy hooted, bending at the waist with laughter.

"It's true," Sara said, blatantly lying. "Stand back and watch."

Caught up in the nonsensical farce, Sara raised herself on tiptoe, planted a big smacking kiss on the palm of her hand, and gave it a Big Bad Wolf huff and puff. She had counted on Crosby's having his nose buried on the computer printouts perpetually cluttering his desk, but she wasn't that lucky. Had the kiss traveled with the speed of a silver bullet, it would have had the same deadly impact. Crosby's body jarred back against his office chair as though making an effort to dodge the imaginary missile.

Oh, cripes, Sara thought, *I've done it again!*

But Crosby didn't fly into a rage and storm out of his office as she expected. He looked . . . stunned. Completely, totally flabbergasted.

Nancy ducked. "I'm getting out of here fast. The pay ain't great, and the fringes are lousy, but I need my job."

"Me, too," Richard said, practically crawling into his neater-than-Mr.-Clean cash drawer in an effort to become invisible.

"I'll protect youse guys," Sara said, bragging with gangster-style bravado, making a cross with her two index fingers. "What do you think Crosby is? The devil reincarnated?"

"Yesssss," both of them replied in unison.

"Cowards," Sara said jeeringly. "You have to be strong! Courageous! Defiant!"

Hunched down, Nancy began shuffling toward the gate out of the tellers' area. "Crazy!" She tossed the word back over her shoulder.

"It helps," Sara muttered to herself.

She ripped off another piece of pretzel and crammed it into her mouth. Inwardly giggling, she tossed Crosby's note into the trash can. She wasn't going to let him intimidate her.

If he wanted a new necktie, she'd get him one. She pictured first a brightly colored, wild striped tie, then a black one with little money wrappers embossed right at the tie tack position. A Hawaiian print would be nice, she mused. Something with big pink hibiscus to clash with the red beam of light coming from his black heart.

Did the color she had painted his heart have anything to do with his lack of response? Sara grimaced. She didn't want to entertain that thought.

Underneath her cap of bubbly curls and her effervescent personality, lay a sensitive core few people saw. Elizabeth Sheffield, her longtime friend, managed to see past the façade of humor, but she ranked among the few.

Sara gritted her teeth behind an engaging smile. *I'd kick my fanny if my foot would reach*, she thought, berating herself. She wanted Ryan Crosby's attention, but not in a derogatory way. In her wildest dreams she featured him bowled over magically by her ready smile, her flirty quips, her . . . ah, hell, Sara mused. The chances of his seeing her as a woman rather than as an extension of the machine she operated would be a million to one. She was better off with his thinking she was a zany broad rather than as someone infatuated with him, she thought, putting everything in proper perspective. He'd get his tie, but she'd have to cover the soft spot in her heart or appear downright roly-poly foolish.

By quitting time Sara could hardly wait to rush out the front door to the nearest department store. She might have to spend her hard-earned cash on replacing his tie, but he'd wish he'd never, ever even thought the word "fat."

Later, a grin of accomplishment on her face, Sara unlocked the door to her apartment and let out a whoop of delight. She had stopped off at Elizabeth Sheffield's apartment next door, explained what had happened, and shown her the tie before going to her own apartment.

The little prank she had played on Elizabeth was cruising along nicely also. During the tumultuous activity at the bank she had forgotten about sending Elizabeth's résumé off, answering Jared McKnight's ad in the *Houston Chronicle* for a "mistress." Her old friend wasn't amused when Sara told her what she'd done, but unless Sara was reading her wrong, Elizabeth anticipated giving Jared McKnight a setdown as much as Sara anticipated her upcoming confrontation with Ryan Crosby.

"Ryan, baby, you're gonna love your new tie!" she said aloud gloatingly, patting the long, narrow box.

She glanced around her condo to make certain everything was in place. The room was decorated in cheerful lemon yellow, accented with splashes of moss green and vibrant aqua. Even gloom and doom Crosby would have trouble bringing his personal rain cloud into this room, she thought with confidence.

After unbuttoning her light-weight jacket, blouse, and skirt, she shimmied out of them while deciding what to wear. Too bad she didn't have a sexy red dress like the one Elizabeth planned to wear for her date with Jared. Or the body to go in it!

She sidestepped the popular trap American women constantly fell into: Starve yourself into a size ten. After all, scratch the surface of a fantastically beautiful woman, and what happened? She'd bleed . . . just like her plump friends.

As Sara showered, washed her hair, and blew it dry, she tried to gain control of her hammering heartbeat. Unwillingly her king-size crush on Ryan Crosby made her heart pound at the thought of having him, alone, in her home. She remembered him when he had first transferred to the bank where they both now worked.

The first three months he worked there he'd been pleasant, friendly, even kind. Certainly an object worthy of hero worship, Sara mused dreamily. What had happened in the last five months to sour him on the human race?

Rumor was he had broken up with his fiancée, but surely one woman couldn't possibly have altered his attitude toward half the world's population. Sara's own love life had had its ups and downs, but she retained her basic happy outlook on life.

Her interest piqued by the slender thread of thought, she wondered if she could add a smidgen of sunlight to his life. The possibility of restoring him to his previous grandeur was a mental as well as physical challenge. Good-humoredly she realized she'd have to carry around a portable stepladder. Otherwise, she'd be kissing his belly button most of the time. But the logistical problem could be overcome, she optimistically reassured herself. The man had to sit down some time during the long night ahead.

The lounging dress she had chosen to wear matched the moss green accessories in her living room. The color seemed to change the golden flecks in her blue eyes to a bright shade of green when she enhanced them with a similar-colored eye shadow. The golden threads that shimmered throughout the fabric accented her unruly curly hair, and the dress displayed a modest amount of cleavage. All in all, Sara was pleased with the overall effect the dress made. A little more at the top and a bit less at the bottom, and she could be a Dolly Parton lookalike.

When she walked into the living room and spotted the Joskey department store package on the end table, she wondered if she had been hasty in her selection of ties. Impulsively she had chosen one which suited his present personality. Maybe she should have chosen something less inflammatory. But when she made the choice, she had been miffed. Pangs of regret coursed through her system.

She headed toward the refrigerator. A gooey cream puff, coated with chocolate sauce, purchased at the best bakery in Houston, immediately caught her attention. Sara didn't have time to exchange her purchase, but she did have enough time to salve her conscience with a few hundred calories.

CHAPTER TWO

Ryan Crosby contemplated the white button under his index finger, hesitating, preparing himself for the unexpected. Sara Hawkins never did the expected. Her business acumen was a distant cousin to her maddening personality. Disconcerted by the unaccustomed grin on his face, he checked his appearance self-consciously.

Dressed in light beige slacks with a matching pullover polo shirt trimmed in white, he scowled as he buttoned the open collar. No point in giving her a buttonhole to target in on with her scissors, he thought. The woman must have experienced temporary insanity when she clipped his tie. He should have fired her on the spot. His climb up the monetary ladder in the banking industry hadn't been accomplished by allowing some crazy twit the privilege of being insubordinate. But if his suspicions were correct, she was skillfully, illegally appropriating small amounts on a regular basis from the People's Bank.

With his own ears he had heard her kid around with customers about taking ten to twenty percent of their deposits. The adage "Where there is smoke there is fire" was applicable. She had certainly made him hot under the collar!

A mask of control slipped over his face. He pressed the doorbell, hoping he wouldn't be greeted with a pie in his puss. There wasn't a doubt in his mind that Sara wouldn't hesitate long enough to think of the consequences. As the door swung open, he automatically tightened his reflexes against any absurd onslaught.

"Ryan," she said warmly, "come in." *You're forty-five seconds late,* she thought, wishing he had totally forgotten about the necktie incident.

Ryan? he thought, forcing himself to enter the lioness's den. *I didn't think she knew my first name.*

Well aware of the disparaging nicknames she had labeled him with, he cautiously glanced at her smiling, upturned face. Undoubtedly she was up to something. He didn't dare take the hand she extended. If he knew her, she probably had one of those electric buzzers hidden in her palm.

Get him off his feet onto his seat, she thought with a speculative gleam in her bright eyes. "Sit down, please. I hate it when you tower over me like a monolith. I'd like to see what the bridge of your nose looks like."

Why don't you insult the man five seconds after he arrives, big mouth? She silently chas-

31

tised herself. There were times in her life when she would have welcomed the uncomfortable feeling of being tongue-tied.

He stared down at the crown of fluffy blond curls and suppressed a grin. Others might say her head was covered with fat curls, but he wouldn't dare. He had stricken the word from his vocabulary as he changed his tie earlier in the day. An unlimited supply of expensive silk ties wasn't in his budget.

"Drink?"

Sara observed his lips momentarily twitching up before they resumed their usual straight line. *Could a smile be lurking in there?* she wondered.

"Tie," he responded curtly.

"Loosen up, Ryan. Have a drink; share a few laughs; then I'll give you your replacement tie," she said in what she hoped was a seductive, coaxing tone.

Ryan wondered what she was up to. Did she suspect he was hot on her heels as the bank's embezzler? Was she going to ply him with liquor in an effort to loosen his tongue? Who did she think she was? Mata Hari? Again his lips began tilting up, but he restrained the impulse to smile. She could hide a wealth of secrets in the cleavage he had observed when he first entered the room.

"Thanks." *Terrific, glib response,* he thought self-chidingly. She wasn't going to let anything slip if he constantly replied with monosyllabic

32

words. "Nice place you have here. Scotch on the rocks, please."

The bottles on the bar clanged together as Sara frantically searched for a bottle of Scotch. To her Scotch tasted like burned rubber, so she seldom bought any. Her eyes scanned over the various bottles containing sloe gin and sweet liqueurs until she spotted a bottle of Chevas Regal a customer had given her as a Christmas present. She filled his request and made herself a sloe gin fizz.

"Here we are," she said, handing him a lowball glass and settling down on the sofa near him.

He hadn't been in this intimate a setting with a woman in months; her nearness made his palms sweat. Sara might be involved in a white-collar crime, but he doubted she was promiscuous. Promiscuity and thievery were different types of immorality. In one long gulp he swallowed the contents of the glass.

"You a closet drinker?" Sara blurted out before thinking. Because she was chagrined at her rude question, a blush tinged her cheeks.

"Thirsty," Ryan uncomfortably explained. "Maybe I'd better have a glass of ice water as a chaser."

He watched Sara nod her head as she rose from the sofa and crossed the room to the bar. The back of his throat burned from the Scotch. The burritos he'd hastily consumed on the way over to her apartment seemed to be stampeding inside his stomach. He had to get her talking to learn anything.

"You've been at the bank a long time, haven't you?"

"Uh-huh. I started working there fresh out of business college." Sara poured him another Scotch and fixed a glass of ice water.

"Why banking?" he inquired once she had returned to the sofa.

She wiggled her light eyebrows and replied, "Some women like the feel of diamonds and furs, but I'm partial to the crisp greenness of U.S. legal tender."

Ryan gulped a swig from the smaller glass she'd placed on the fruitwood coffee table. "Other people's money excites you?" he queried, certain he was on the right track.

Laughing, Sara took a sip of the creamy pink liquid in her glass. "I manage to survive on my earnings," she replied, gesturing toward the quality of interior decorating in her home. "I'm not a high roller. But there is money to be made in banking."

"You must manage your money carefully to live in this condo, dress as well as you do, and lavishly furnish your home." His dark eyes steadfastly locked on to her pleased expression.

Sara shrugged, a warm tingle circuiting through her nervous system. Let him think she was a wise money manager. She wouldn't let on that her father had bought the condo as a graduation present or that she was an only child whose mother still lavished presents on her.

34

"I've been around the bank a long time. Watching the experts operate helps."

Helps do what? he wanted to ask. *Helps you figure out a way to siphon enough cash to pay for the extras I know you can't afford? Helps you plan the perfect crime?* The sweet, trusting smile on her lips, edged with a teeny pink mustache from her drink, didn't fool him. But it did make him want to kiss some sense into her bubblehead. If she would confess, he would make certain the authorities went easy on her. His chest muscles tightened at the thought of Sara's going to prison. He scowled at his own reaction. A thief belonged behind bars . . . and not the kind of bars found in the turn-of-the-century tellers' cages.

Sara felt a shaft of anticipation when she realized he wanted to kiss her. She knew he was unaware of his masculine body leaning toward her. He seemed totally captivated. Provocatively she let the tip of her tongue remove the froth from the fizz on the corners of her mouth. He was close enough for her to smell his subtle aftershave cologne, so Sara smoothly set her drink on the table. She didn't want to distract him from the mesmerizing web she had drawn him into by dumping a cold drink in his lap.

"Your face is very expressive," Ryan murmured, wondering how she managed to conceal her deceitfulness with such a beatific smile.

Her inviting lips enticed him to come closer, to touch, explore, taste their sweetness. Silently they promised to take him past reason, past sus-

35

picion, past doubts. His hands gently moved to caress her rounded shoulders. Her acquiescent softness jolted him. He'd been deceived by one woman's enchanting promises. Only a fool would succumb to Sara's seduction. He suspected her of thievery. Yet he also realized Sara Hawkins was the first woman he had wanted to kiss since Susan had broken their engagement.

He forced himself to peel his fingers one by one off her shoulders. Susan had taught him an invaluable lesson about women, about himself. He wasn't going to risk falling for a woman he suspected had fewer ethics than his former fiancée possessed. Proving himself strong by resisting her, he also managed to sip from his drink without exposing his shaky hands.

Sara's reaction to his abrupt withdrawal was involuntary: Her stomach growled loudly. Automatically she reached for the end table, opened the drawer, and pulled out a box of Cheezits. Perplexed, disappointed, she crammed a handful of the square objects into her mouth.

Crunching her munchies, she tried to figure out what had gone wrong. Mindful of her manners, Sara held the box out to Ryan. When he refused with a curt shake of his head, she plummeted her small hand back into the box for another handful.

"So," Ryan said, starting where their conversation had ended, "you've been with the bank several years. I guess your reputation of being trustworthy and loyal has been earned."

Mouth full, Sara bobbed her head up and

36

down. The man was schizo. One minute he was on the verge of kissing her, next he turned away as though spinach were dangling from between her front teeth, and then he spouted a litany about how wonderful an employee she was. Sara swallowed, clearing her mouth of food.

"You've earned your reputation, too," she said.

He slowly rose to his feet, and drink still in hand, he crossed to the window. Daylight savings time had extended the hours of sunlight. Although the horizon's colors were a splendid pinkish orange, the sun clung to the blue heavens. One hand on his hip, his back to Sara, he answered, suddenly weary, "Humbug Crosby? No-Sense-of-Humor Crosby? Stick-in-the-Mud Crosby?"

"I didn't call you a stick-in-the-mud," Sara protested, confirming her guilt in being the originator of the other nicknames. The hand she clamped over her mouth smelled of cheddar cheese. Under other conditions she would have inhaled deeply, enjoying the aroma, but she felt nauseated instead. "You could smile once in a while to let us know you're human."

Ever so slowly Ryan pivoted on the ball of his foot. The grotesque twisting of his lips couldn't be classified as a smile by any standards. "Like this?"

Sara brushed the crumbs off her lap. "That's not exactly what I had in mind. More like this," she said, giving him an ear-to-ear grin that didn't quite reach her eyes.

Determined to make him laugh, Sara scrambled to her feet and closed the distance between them. Might as well be fired for molestation than for insubordination, she rationalized. Her short fingers dug into his ribs and climbed up and down their taut surface. She giggled when she saw him flinch and start to move away. Her head cocked to hear his first burst of laughter, she busily strummed on his rib cage. She heard nothing, not even a quiet chuckle.

"I'm not ticklish," he soberly informed her.

"Goosey?" she asked, willing to go to any limits to make him laugh.

"Dead ass," he replied, a trace of a smile in his mind at her audacious question.

"How about pain? I could make you a hair shirt or beat you with a silk-tasseled whip," she said. Her mind churned out scandalous suggestions; her unrestricted mouth babbled them as she cheekily smiled.

His brown eyes visibly hardened. "There are no boundaries to your disgraceful behavior, are there?"

"Okay . . . nothing kinky," she said. "How about—"

"Give up, Sara. And for heaven's sake, wipe the Cheezits off your mouth!"

"You could kiss them off," she suggested with determination glinting from her eyes. "You wanted to kiss me earlier."

Exasperated with himself, Ryan couldn't deny her allegation. "The tie and an apology will suffice."

"You'd like a kiss better," she said. "Who knows? Maybe the only time your lips curve up is when they are being touched by mine. Let's give it a try."

"Sara!"

"Jeez, Ryan, you're acting like a reluctant virgin. Come on, big fella, pucker up, here comes a big one." The more Ryan protested, the more spunky she became. She locked one arm around his waist to prevent him from escaping and thumped his heart with her fist. "Are you in there, heart? Listen up. Get ready for a dynamite blast of adrenaline. You aren't dead! There isn't any tombstone at Ryan's head."

Ryan tried to extricate himself, but Sara clung tenaciously. "Don't be ridiculous," he gasped, his body immediately responding to her womanly softness.

"Bend down here, mountain man, or I'm going to unbuckle your pants and you'll have to go home half-naked," she said threateningly, steadfastly holding him in her clutches.

"You wouldn't!"

Sara raised her head and arched one eyebrow.

"You would," Ryan said. "This is preposterous. A woman isn't supposed to tackle a man and demand a kiss. Next, you'll—"

"I haven't thought about *next*. We'll see how the kiss goes," she replied, sensing he was weakening. "I'm going to count to three. Then I'm going to—"

He didn't give her time to finish the threat. Shoulders hunching, he wrapped his arms around Sara, struggled to lift her off her feet, and fervently began kissing her.

Sara expected eventual capitulation, but she was unprepared for the mastery of his kiss, which made him the victor. When she felt his lips hungrily devouring hers, her heartbeat accelerated as though she had thumped her own chest. Feet dangling inches from the floor, she clung to his shoulders, relishing his strength, his dominance. She had badgered him into kissing her, but the electrical impulses vibrating, humming like high-voltage wires throughout her bloodstream justified her death-defying actions.

Her smiling lips parted to invite further intimacy. The chuckle of delight contained in the back of her throat changed to a sweet moan when he skillfully flicked the tip of his tongue over her taste buds. Sweet, sour, salty explosions occurred. Nothing she had ever eaten satisfied her more than his sensual probing. Greedily she sipped, begging for more.

Ryan had intended to give her a quick peck, demand his tie, and make a hasty departure. But the second their bodies tangled, any thought of a rapid retreat vanished. Pent-up sexual urges he hadn't experienced in months surged through his wiry frame, settling below his belt buckle with fiery heat. He pressed against the undersoftness of her belly, relishing a glorious masculine surge. His tongue probed back and forth, swirling, synchronized with the quick thrusts of his hips. He wanted Sara Hawkins. He wanted her with an aching need of a man long denied a loving woman.

For once in her life Sara was shocked. The strangled low moans she heard excited and repelled her at the same time. Had she created a sexual Frankenstein? One moment she was pestering him for a kiss, the next he had her in a lover's grip, swiftly followed by the unmistakable sign of his arousal. Although her body responded with an aching hollowness in the pit of her stomach, she knew his overwhelming reaction to her wasn't due to any mutual tender feelings. Ryan wanted her physically, but a quick release for their sexual needs without emotional commitment wasn't enough for Sara. Two people who shared the ultimate intimacies should care about each other. Anything less was repugnant. Bedhopping wasn't a chapter in her code of ethical behavior book.

She unhooked her fingers from around his neck. With a final flick of regret, she closed her mouth and withdrew. Ryan held her in a bone-crushing embrace as he strung hot, moist kisses over her cheekbones. Again and again he returned to her lips.

"Ryan," she gasped, trying to ignore her own clamoring senses, "we're acting like a couple of sex maniacs. Stop." Her uncurbed tongue voiced her thoughts.

"No. Tell me you want me as much as I want you," he muttered against her ear as he made quick forays with his lips.

41

Sara denied his claim. "You want a body . . . *any* body."

"Don't tease, Sara. I'm practically shaking with need. Isn't that enough?"

"No," she replied weakly. "I'm not . . . loose."

A harsh laugh accompanied her immediate release. Sara swallowed convulsively when she stepped backward. Every horror story about sexual violence she had read in the newspaper or seen on television flashed in front of her widened eyes. Her knees threatened to buckle beneath her weight.

Ryan fought for control of his passion, his anger, his shame. The skin, tight across his cheekbones, refused to relax. But with visible effort, he unclenched his hands when he saw the terror in Sara's eyes. She didn't know she had released emotions he had thought long deceased. *She doesn't know . . . and I can't tell her. Better to leave her petrified than to trade terror for pity.*

"You can laugh about this at the bank tomorrow. Throw a few more kisses in my direction when you're bored. Or maybe, since you don't have an inhibited bone in your body, you could strip down and traipse through my office. That should make everyone laugh." The hoarseness of his voice grated against his ears.

"I'm sorry. I didn't mean . . ."

"Sorry?" Ryan hooted. "You aren't sorry about leading me on any more than you're sorry about hacking off my tie."

Ryan loomed over her, but she felt shorter

than her normal size. A toothpick would have been taller.

"Give me the tie, and I'll get the hell out of here before you burst into gales of laughter."

"I'm not laughing," Sara mumbled. Her head dropped as she retreated to get the narrow package. "You aren't going to like what I bought. Let me pick out another one tomorrow."

"Oh, no, Sara Hawkins. Your passionate kiss paid the price of having the last laugh. You're entitled."

"I don't want it. Before you came over, I thought I could bring a little sunshine into your life. Make you happy," she confessed, wanting him to understand her motives for demanding a kiss.

"Forget the pity. I don't need it. Feel sorry for some other poor sucker you're going to lead down the garden path."

A burst of defiance bubbled out of her mouth before she could stop its flow. "I didn't lead you anywhere. You took the initiative . . . just like when you insinuated I'm fat. How do you think you made me feel?"

The wounded expression on her face hurt Ryan more than her refusal to go to bed with him. An inner struggle tugged at his heart. He readily admitted to himself the remark he'd made at the bank was off base. But dammit, she laughed and joked about her weight with everyone else at work. How was he supposed to know

43

his offhand comment would light the fuse on the bomb that had just gone off?

"About as lousy as I feel right now," he mumbled aloud.

He raked his hand through his dark hair. She deserved an apology, but the words stuck in his throat. Months ago, after Susan's desertion, he promised himself he'd never let any woman get under his skin. But he had. His dark eyes raked over Sara Hawkins's rounded curves. *Damn you,* he wanted to shout. *Don't make me feel! I'm better off encased in a coffin than being wounded again.*

The admission to himself of the effect she had on him left him dumb struck. How had she managed to make him forget the reason for his being in her apartment to begin with? *Her craziness must be infectious,* he thought. *And plenty of bed rest isn't the cure!*

"Forget the tie. I don't want anything from you."

Sara flinched as though struck. Hurt quickly changed to anger, oiling her rapier tongue. "Well, Mr. Neck-Longer-Than-a-Giraffe's, I wouldn't consider reneging on a suitable replacement for the tie I ruined."

She wanted him out of her home, out of her personal life. Her short legs swiftly carried her to the front door via the table she had placed the package on. Tears gathering in the corners of her eyes, she swung the door open.

"Here's your blankety-blank tie. Wear it in good health!" She glanced out into the summer's

44

darkness, which had quickly blanketed the condo project once the sun had set. "There's supposed to be a full moon tonight. Go find yourself another woman. You are one weird wolf!"

Ryan took the slender box from her extended hand. They both were better off if she thought he was a monster. Neither of them would be hurt as long as anger lay between them. The sheen of moisture coating her blue eyes was of the same substance as the knot clogging his throat. Sadly he shook his head.

"Good night, Sara," he whispered. Remorse made him add, "Sweet dreams."

"Nightmares if you're in them!"

She slammed the door, gulping down salty tears. In a protective gesture she crossed her arms over her chest. Her chin thrust upward, she absolutely refused to cry. Twin tears slid from the outside edges. Defensively she forced a grin on her face. *Laugh, you fool, don't cry!* she thought, berating herself. But laughter wouldn't come. The dark, gloomy cloud Ryan Crosby carried around with him rained down her cheeks. Instead of bringing sunshine into his life, he had brought tears into hers.

CHAPTER THREE

Sara ended up mentally replaying the disastrous episode throughout the weekend. Normally she'd have confided her problems to Elizabeth, but her friend had her own problems with Jared McKnight. At noon on Saturday the two women decided to drown their sorrows with salt water and head for the Galveston beach. But the mind-diverting trip was aborted when Jared arrived, a long-stemmed red rose in hand and a humble apology on his lips. Elizabeth had gaily traipsed off to Galveston with Jared instead of with Sara. Maybe Sara would have been able to forget about Ryan had she tagged along with Elizabeth. Perhaps finding some uncomplicated hunk of beach flesh would have been less worrisome than fretting about Ryan nonstop for two days.

On Monday, back in her teller's cage, a smile spread over her face as she licked the end of the money strap and carefully aligned the wrapper before sealing it closed. Over the long weekend Sara had made to herself several promises she fully intended to keep. Prior to the confrontation with Ryan she'd considered working in the bank as just a job. She'd collected her paycheck each Friday, knowing she'd earned it, but her shortsighted goals hadn't been career-oriented. But now she envisioned herself as an officer of the bank. That should get Ryan Crosby's attention.

Zany behavior was inappropriate for the future vice-president of the People's Bank. She would conduct herself in a judicious manner, right down from the dark conservative suit she wore to the wedged heels on her feet. Her demeanor would reflect the seriousness of her career goals. If she couldn't establish and maintain a relationship with an unmarried man, she would set her mind on getting a promotion.

The vow to keep a civil tongue in her head would be the hardest to keep. But if necessary, she would have her jaws wired shut to accomplish the feat. Nothing and nobody, including Mr. Ryan Crosby, would ignite her tongue into misbehaving. Never again, she solemnly promised herself, would she string together a phrase with hyphens instead of using Mr. Crosby's correct title.

Sara closed her reorganized drawer and reached into the brown grocery bag that contained her lunch. Her eyes staring straight ahead, she snitched a strawberry from the plastic container. Hiding it in the palm of her hand, she raised it to her mouth. The taste of tart sweetness flooding her taste buds brought a sigh

of satisfaction. When she had repeatedly recon-
structed and listed her crimes against acting like
a professional, she had quickly drawn a line
through her tendency to snack. How could she
possibly live up to the restrictions she had
placed on herself and not eat? Impossible. As the
Greeks had said, everything in moderation. She
would watch what she ate, bite by bite, and enjoy each morsel passing between her lips.

Determined to make a fresh start with Ryan,
she had spent Saturday afternoon searching for
a tie any Birchite would be proud to wear. Before she had begun her official duties of the day,
she had slipped into Ryan's office and left it on
his desk as a peace offering. Saying she was sorry
wasn't enough. She would prove to him that she
could be . . . stuffy.

"Good morning, Mr. Kent. How's the best
boutique in Houston faring?" she said, greeting
one of her favorite customers.

"Fine, Sara. From the looks of what you're
wearing today, I'd say you need to come check
the clothes racks for yourself," he said lightly,
sniffing in polite distaste at her drab garments.
"Perhaps you could salvage your sackcloth look
with a brightly colored scarf."

"Scarves are passé," she replied scoffingly.

"Nothing is out of fashion with the exception
of being poorly dressed. A bluish green scarf
would accent your face, highlight those spar-
kling eyes."

"Flatterer," she answered. She glanced at the

quarterly savings statement in his hand and inquired, "Is there a problem with your account?"

Mr. Kent rubbed his smoothly shaven jaw thoughtfully. "I'm not certain."

Sara took the sheet and turned it toward her. "I don't see anything out of order. According to this, you made a few small withdrawals, and a few days later you made deposits bringing the balance up to the original amount."

"Oh, the balance is right," he said readily, "but I didn't make any withdrawals or deposits."

Puzzled, Sara glanced from the savings statement to his face. "No activity on the account. Something doesn't make sense. Why don't you let me check out the microfiche and get back to you?"

"I'd appreciate it. Since it's the shop's company account with my assistant's signature on the card, maybe . . ."

"No, I don't believe Crissy would . . ."

"Steal?" He shook his head. "I don't want to accuse anybody of juggling the books, but if there are discrepancies, I need to know about it."

"I'm certain I'll be able to unlock the mystery for you. It may take a couple of days to track down the original withdrawal and deposit slips since I'll have to go to the files sent to the main bank, but don't worry. I'm certain it's just a silly mixup." She grinned to reassure him.

"I hope so. Good employees are hard to come by in Boomtown, U.S.A. Crissy may have a financial problem she's covering up," he said, his hand rubbing his brow.

"Frowns grow wrinkles," she blurted out, then bit her tongue, so she wouldn't complete the rest of the sentence. The head teller shouldn't tell a customer he was going to resemble a prune if he kept worrying.

"Give me a call when you've found out who signed those slips, will you?"

"Yes, sir. As soon as I know what happened, you'll hear from me," she told him.

"Thanks, Sara." His eyes flicked over her attire for one final inspection. "Come on over to the boutique, and I'll personally supervise future additions to your wardrobe, okay?"

"Do you really think the suit is horrible?" she asked, fingering the mannish lapel.

"Yeah. Makes you look like the Goodyear blimp in mourning," he said jovially. "Those sweet feminine curves should be accented, not draped."

Omar the tentmaker, she privately joked, her personal clothing designer, must have been moonlighting as a funeral director, she almost sassed Mr. Kent, but didn't. She chuckled to let Mr. Kent know she wasn't offended and kept her smart mouth shut.

Once Mr. Kent had entered the safety-deposit box area, she reexamined the statement. Had Crissy been dabbling in the company account? She shook her head negatively. But then, if not Crissy, who? Worrying her lower lip with her front teeth, she rebelled against the other possibilities. Thoughtfully she raised her blue eyes and scanned the faces of the other three tellers. Could one of them be responsible?

She knew each of them well and immediately rejected the idea. None of them to her knowledge was in desperate need of some ready cash. Kate Davis, wife of a prosperous attorney, worked rather than keep house. Marge Cranson, wife of a plastic surgeon, dispensed money as a teller because in some strange way it satisfied her craving to do charity work. And timid, reclusive Richard Grant would die of a heart attack if anyone near him stole a penny and he found out about it. Then who? Who, other than the four tellers, had access to the paper work?

A shudder ran up her spine. *Not him, not Ryan,* she thought, stoutly denying the other option.

Unwillingly her wild imagination took control. What were the first clues one looked for when seeking out an embezzler? No absenteeism, she answered silently, remembering an article she had read in a trade magazine. Ryan Crosby's attendance record was perfect. The tellers had joked about letting their hair down and romping through the bank if he ever took a day off.

Fluctuating swings of mood was another clue she had read about in a banking magazine. He didn't fit into that mold. Or did he? Hadn't he switched from amorous lover to Mr. Priggish-Petunia without batting an eyelash?

Sara bent down to get another strawberry.

The tart juice stung the small abrasion she had inflicted on her lip when she had bitten it.

Sneaky, shifty eyes, she thought, calling up the detective story she had watched on television the previous night. All stereotypical criminals had squinty eyes. Mentally she envisioned Ryan's dark brown eyes. They were gorgeous when he wasn't angry, she mused, striking the eyes clue from her list.

Marge has squinty eyes. Says she's nearsighted. Ha! Too shortsighted to see the consequences of pilfering other people's money? Could it be sweet Marge was playing Robin Hood and stealing from the savings accounts to give to the needy? Sara shook her head. Marge wasn't the type. But who was?

She glanced at the clock over the new accounts officer's desk. The small hand was on the ten and the long hand on the three. Was Ryan going to be absent from work? Fervently she hoped so. Out of the three clues his attendance record was the most incriminating.

No such luck, she thought as she saw him coming through the double glass doors.

Her eyes widened. He was smiling a real smile. Her jaw dropping, she couldn't believe her eyes. She blinked several times to make certain she wasn't reliving the nightmare that had haunted her sleep. A low, guttural moan hummed behind the jaw she snapped shut. "He's wearing it. He's wearing the tie!" she whispered, panicking.

To the casual observer the tie appeared to be

a conservative brown strip of quality silk with squiggles and tiny blue letters making an overall design. On closer inspection Sara knew the viewer would see the letters *MCP*, and the blurred design was actually piglets. She could have branded MALE CHAUVINIST PIG on his forehead, and it would have been as subtle as the tie he wore.

While Ryan went from desk to desk and greeted the office staff with a beaming smile and a friendly hello, Sara plopped the NEXT WINDOW PLEASE sign on the counter and dashed toward his office. Didn't he know what *MCP* stood for? He'd be the laughingstock of the bank within an hour.

Skidding to a halt outside his office door, she watched him chat with the attractive woman the bank had recently hired for its new promotion scheme. Sara wanted to hide behind the potted palm when the woman reached up and touched the replacement tie.

The part of her that didn't want to hide wanted to slap the woman's hand. Where did she get off touching the vice-president, in broad daylight, practically in the middle of the lobby? If she laid a smackaroo on his lips, Sara would shred her pantyhose! She didn't stop to analyze her reaction, but her eyes danced with fiery green sparks.

"Good morning, Sara." Ryan amiably greeted her as he strode past her into his office.

Sara followed him in and shut the door. "Take

that off," she demanded, ready to assist him if he refused.

"I like it . . . and the person who gave it to me," he softly replied in a voice Sara barely recognized. He eased back in his chair, relaxed.

"Wear this one," Sara instructed as she opened the box on his desk and raised a striped tie for him to inspect.

"Boring," he commented. "Everyone thinks this one is—"

"Take it off," she said, slowly enunciating the command as though his brains were on the floor instead of inside his head.

"What are you going to take off?" Ryan said teasingly. "Turnabout is fair play."

"Don't be absurd," Sara said admonishingly.

"Why? Two absurd people in one bank make a crowd?" he replied.

"Look, Mr.—" She almost said "Not-So-Bright-About-Interpreting-Initials," but remembering her recently made vow about hyphenated titles, she substituted "Crosby" and added, "Your clothing reflects what you are, who you are." She watched him agree by nodding his head. *If he'd get the cocky, lopsided smile off his face, I'd know his ears are functioning,* she thought, her own lips forming a thin line. "The tie conflicts with your image."

Deliberately Ryan widened his grin and accented the move by tracing his finger of the broad curve his lower lip made. "I owe my new image to you. The traumatic experience I had months ago shouldn't have jaded my outlook on

54

life. Thank goodness you tornadoed your way into my life and changed all that."

"Fine. Super," she commented, intent on getting her offensive gift from underneath his collar. "Now, change your tie."

"Sara, you aren't listening to me." He softly reprimanded her. "The tie makes people smile. Weren't you the one, using every imaginable trick in the joke book, who told me to smile? Well? The tie makes me smile, and everyone who sees it smiles also. I spread twenty-four hours of sunshine in the time it took me to greet everyone today."

"They aren't smiling *with* you; they are smiling *at* you," she pointed out.

"Ah, everyone smiling but you upsets your equilibrium? Maybe Miss Glorious-Sunshine will smile if I kiss her," he said contemplatively. He braced his hands on the desk and began levering himself to his feet.

"Don't you dare," Sara squawked and retreated two steps. "It's daytime, you're at the bank—"

"How do you feel about skinny, tall men, Sara?" Ryan circled from behind his desk, closing the gap.

Her head swiveled from side to side as she glanced from the plate glass separating the rest of the bank from his office to the man stalking her. She spotted Mr. Kent waving in her direction as he walked toward the front doors.

Ominously she issued a threat she knew he would understand. "I know what you're up to, and it won't work. You can't keep my mouth shut by—"

"Wrong. I can quite effectively shut you up."

Sara tried to wriggle out of his arms, but they were clamped around her like a rubber band on a stack of money. The more she wiggled, the more tightly he embraced her and the wider he smiled.

"I'll release you, Miss Concerned-About-What-People-Will-Think, when you promise to go out to dinner with me."

"Never," she said as she jabbed him in the rib cage with one pointed fingernail. "You can't be trusted."

"I'm reformed, remember?"

She jerked her head up, away from the busy piglets on his tie. "Do you mean it? You won't take any more—"

"Nothing. Unless you are an equal participant," he said softly.

One thing he had learned over the weekend during the hours he walked the Galveston beach was that he had a special feeling for Sara Hawkins, and he was going to do everything within his power to gain her confidence. He couldn't believe she was the petty thief, but he'd protect her if he could.

"Can you afford to take me out?" she asked with concern. "You aren't under money pressures, are you?"

Ryan captured the thick blond curls at her nape and buried his long fingers into them. Was she expressing her own plight? His dark eyes bore into her worried blue eyes. "I make twice your salary. You aren't short on cash, are you?"

"Of course not," she said huffily. Jeez, he was the one taking the bank's money. What was he going to do? Lend her some of his ill-gotten gains?

"You'll come to me if you are, won't you?" he asked, pressing her face against his chest, his heart.

"I'd go to the loan officer first. My bank account is fat and sassy. How about yours?"

"Lean and mean . . . the way I was before you came into my life. But I can afford a modest meal. Seven o'clock agreeable?"

The triumphant chuckle she heard sent shivers to each point where his body touched hers. She needed time to reform him, convince him of the erroneous path down which his sticky fingers were taking him. She accepted with a nod.

Ryan moved away inch by inch, reluctant to let her out of his arms for any reason. "Wear something pretty," he whispered, taking a step back.

"You aren't partial to black and white?" she asked, thinking how poorly he would look in a prisoner's stripes.

"I'm partial to you," he replied, his tone full of meaning. "I owe you for bringing me to my senses."

With a cheeky grin Sara quipped, "I'll look forward to collecting your IOU in person."

The expression on her mobile face would

57

have perplexed the other employees had they noticed her as she left his office. Although her brow pleated down, her lips curved up into a smile that would have rivaled the happy face stickers used to seal the bank's statements. She felt as though her heart were in her mouth, and it didn't taste good.

"He didn't do it," she muttered to herself. "You jumped to the wrong conclusion." She repeated her statement, firmly, instructing herself to believe it. Kate, she thought, searching for anyone other than Ryan as the guilty party.

When Kate smiled at her as though she had heard Sara thinking her name, Sara ducked her head. She couldn't ponder ugly thoughts and grin at the person she mentally defiled. It wasn't Kate. It wasn't Richard. It wasn't Marge. *Well,* she thought with a grimace after narrowing down the choices, *I guess I'm the only one left.*

But she knew she hadn't committed any crime. Was Ryan the guilty party?

Because she did not want to think about Ryan's guilt, her windy imagination whipped through her brain as she contemplated what she would have done if she had stolen the money. A trip to Hawaii would be fun. All those grass skirts, leis, and golden brown skins might be worth ten years to life in prison. Or perhaps a safari to Africa, with a daring hunter leading the way through the darkened jungle.

Her vivid imagination blew at gale force when the courageous hunter turned around and she saw Ryan Crosby grinning, winking, beckoning her into a grass hut. The throbbing beat of her heart rivaled the volume of primitive native drums. Yes, indeed, she mused dreamily, twenty minutes in a grass hut with Ryan Crosby would be worth twenty years of being anywhere else.

A few minutes later she held the odious statement in her hands and forgot about the fantasies the extra money would buy. Within twenty-four hours she would know for certain who the thief was. But did she want to know? Sara resolutely picked up the phone and dialed the number of the records department. At the same time she reached into the brown sack and covertly munched on another strawberry as she asked for the needed information. When she hung the phone up, she prayed her suspicions were wrong. For a person who prided herself on being right the prayer was a big concession.

Ryan watched her carefully. There was almost a rhythm to her bobbing up and down in the teller's cage. What was she doing? Exercising? Or stealthily tucking twenties into her purse? He rubbed his forehead vigorously as though he could blot out his suspicions by easing the wrinkles on his forehead.

The Academy Awards would be received by less consummate actors than he had been. The computer sheets didn't lie, unless the person programming the information was a liar. Someone, Sara being the most likely, had managed to break the fail-safe code every Impact card holder had: his or her pin number. Someone— again Sara was on top of the suspicion list—had managed to get the card, find out the pin number, use the card for a short time, dabbling with small amounts and replacing them, and had accomplished the feat without detection.

Until he, purely by accident, had discovered activity on generally nonactive accounts, the embezzler had had free access to thousands of dollars. As long as the books balanced at the end of the month, when the trials were run on the savings accounts, and as long as the sums were undetected by the depositors, she remained safe. But how long could her luck hold?

Ryan pinched his lips between his thumb and index finger. The truth would come out, but he didn't want it to pass from his lips. It would be idiotic to believe he could persuade Sara to turn herself in. She'd turn tail toward South America to evade prosecution.

Overdramatic, Ryan thought, scoffing at himself. A criminal didn't have to leave the country to escape being sent to the pen. All she had to do was lie low in a metropolitan area like Houston. Look at how many illegal aliens managed to remain in Texas without benefit of green cards.

"You're rationalizing," Ryan whispered aloud. "You're interested in the woman, not the embezzler." She had accomplished the impossible. She had given him back his heart.

And what was he going to do to return the favor? Why, have her locked up, of course. But his idea of a date wasn't a visiting permit to the local federal penitentiary.

He realized he had muttered the words for

anyone outside his office door to hear and clamped his mouth into a straight line. The supreme folly would be to cover up her unscrupulous deeds and have someone overhear him talking to himself.

There had to be a way to convince Sara she didn't need the little extras in life. Then, and only then, would he be able to convince her to curb her monetary appetite. Heck, he'd recommend a promotion and pay raise to keep her from recklessly chancing being discovered. His thoughts paused as he asked himself an important question: How far would he go to cover up for an embezzler?

His eyes watched Sara duck down again. He jumped to his feet as though they were on opposite ends of a seesaw. When she straightened, he sat back down. He couldn't see what she was doing beneath the counter regardless of how hard he tried. She looked guilty as hell when her eyes darted from one side of the bank to the other. Her hand covered her mouth. Was she putting money in her mouth and spitting it into her purse as she bent down?

Unorthodox as the method seemed, it appeared logical. Ryan fought the urge to rush out and tape her mouth closed until he could convince her she was digging her way into jail with her own mouth.

He flipped the computer sheets on his desk to the daily savings activity. The process of noting withdrawals from inactive accounts proved to be a long, tedious job, but Ryan had set his mind to compiling a list the embezzler would be unable to deny. He knew the money was taken and replaced through the Impact system, but for the life of him, he couldn't discover how the embezzler managed to get the card and the pin number. Sara needed them both to get into a customer's account. Determined to have all the information, he jotted down the name of an account that during the past month had shown unaccustomed activity.

Tonight, he promised himself, *tonight I'll find out exactly how she does it.*

Sara breezed into the customer service department with purposeful steps. Much as she hated herself for snooping into Ryan's account, she couldn't get rid of the nagging doubts plaguing her. She had already looked his account number up in the files. Now all she had to do was feed the information into the computer and receive a printout. But first she had to get rid of Sharon, the employee who took care of customer requests.

Beaming a wide smile in Sharon's direction, Sara nervously flicked the scrap of paper with Ryan Crosby's account number on it. "Sharon, why don't you take a break? I've screwed up my checking account, and I need to get a printout. While I'm waiting, I'll take care of the counter."

"Not you, too!" Sharon moaned. "I swear, bank employees are the absolute worst about balancing their checkbooks! I'll run it," she said, stretching out her hand for the innocuous-looking slip of paper.

Sara squirmed on her three-inch stacked heels. Laughing squeakily, she shook her head. "You'd be shocked at the depleted condition of my bank account," she said, racking her brain for a means of getting to the machine without letting Sharon know she was playing detective.

"You're not overdrawn, are you?"

"Maybe." She hung her head as though embarrassed. "Really, Sharon, I'd rather do it myself."

Sharon wrapped her arm around Sara's shoulder and gave her a slight squeeze. "I'll just grab a cup of coffee while you're busy."

"Thanks. One more favor, please. Don't mention this to anyone, okay?"

"My lips are sealed," Sharon answered, swiping her finger across them before she grinned and began walking toward the lunchroom.

Not wasting a moment, Sara keyed in the number. Impatient to find out if corresponding deposits had been made in his account, Sara bent over the printout machine and avidly watched the numbers being printed out. Nothing appeared to be out of the ordinary. Every month there was a deposit, throughout the month checks were drawn on the account. She sighed, relieved.

But wait a minute, she thought. *Only a stupid fool would deposit stolen money into a checking account. He'd put it . . . where? A Swiss bank,* she answered, remembering the plot of a recent detective program she'd seen. Or maybe he had a fictitious bank account under another name.

Or possibly a safety-deposit box. His options were limitless. And there wouldn't be any way in the world she could track his money down.

Sara ripped the perforated sheet off the roll, and she jumped when she heard Ryan's voice from the other side of the customer counter.

"What are you doing in customer service?" Ryan asked, noticing that she wadded the sheet of paper she'd removed from the printer and stuck it behind her back.

"Uh, uh," Sara stammered, stalling for an inspired reply. The incriminating evidence behind her back would incur his wrath more than the pair of scissors had. A whopping lie popped into her mind. "Checking my account to see if the Good Fairy deposited my oil money."

"Oil money?"

"Yeah, uh, I have her deposit the money directly," she said. "You didn't know you had a date tonight with an oil heiress, did you? Guess you'll have to take me someplace fancy since you've found out the source of my private income." A weak, wobbly grin aimed in his direction, she hoped, would lend credence to the blatant lie.

Ryan chuckled to cover his disbelief. "Every Texan owns at least one oil well."

"I'm native-born. I own a whole oilfield," she said, stretching the lie to the hilt. "What are you doing here?"

"Following you. Hoping you'd head toward the bank vault," he answered glibly. "I thought

I'd see if you taste as good in the morning as you do in the evening."

Her knees threatening to buckle at the husky, seductive tone in his voice, Sara leaned her shoulder against the counter. "Shush your mouth. Someone will hear you."

"We have nothing to hide, do we?" His brown eyes moved from her eyes to the hand she kept hidden behind her back.

The wad of paper burned like a hot, molten rock in her hand. Slowly she brought it in front of her ample bustline. Oh, how she wished she could stuff the incriminating evidence in her mouth and swallow. *Why not?* she thought. He expected outrageous conduct from her, didn't he?

"Ever taste this printer paper? Delicious," she confided as she ripped off the top part with his name on it and crammed it into her mouth.

Her taste buds revolted against the disgusting taste and threatened to reject the obnoxious offering. Sara forced herself to chew and smile at the same time. She ripped off the blank end of the paper and handed it to Ryan.

"Want some?" she asked. The attempt to swallow almost defeated her tongue. "A bit dry but chewy."

Ryan realized she was bit by bit destroying evidence of her crime, but he felt helpless to stop her. "You'll get sick."

Damned right. She mentally blasted herself but continued to smile while she tore off another strip at the top of the statement and shoved it inside her cheek.

"Must have a billy goat in my family closet. I love paper." She munched down on the wad, shifting it to the other side. "When I was a kid, I ate reams of notebook paper. Sure you don't want some?"

"No," Ryan said. The bliss written on her face made his stomach flop over. "Don't fill up before tonight," he cautioned.

Sara swallowed. *Through the lips, over the tongue, watch out, stomach, here it comes,* she warned herself. Her stomach churned in response to the abuse.

Ryan watched her shovel in another piece of paper and decided to be merciful before she ate the entire sheet. "Since you won't venture with me to the bank vault, I'd better get back to my desk."

He started to turn away, then halted. "You have to promise me one thing if I take you to an expensive restaurant."

"What's that?"

"Don't eat the menu!" he said, chuckling at his own joke.

The paper inside her mouth seemed to double in size. Sara bobbed her head up and down, raised her finger, and crossed her heart. Speech was impossible.

She waited until he was out of sight to stick her head into an empty metal wastepaper basket. Mouth dry, stomach close to civil war, she provided an antidote to the sickening feeling by

66

gulping air. A belch that would have made the blast of a roaring cannon jealous detonated against her eardrums. Sara immediately extracted her head and shook it to eliminate the ringing sensation in her ears.

"You sick?" Sharon asked, concerned.

"Something caught in my throat. It's out now," she answered, straightening.

"My bank statement makes me sick, too," Sharon excused. "Thank God we get paid Friday."

"Another day older and deeper in debt?" Sara asked in a sing-along voice.

"Right on. I'm lucky I don't have to handle the money you do or I'd be singing the 'Folsom Prison Blues.'"

Her blue eyes narrowing suspiciously, Sara wondered if Sharon could be the embezzler. She laughed appropriately at Sharon's attempt at humor and rejected the possibility of her being the thief.

"Thanks for the printout," Sara said as she headed toward the swinging gate in the counter.

Sara returned to her cage to study the part of the statement she hadn't eaten. There had to be a clue she had missed in her quick survey of his monthly account. But there wasn't.

She'd get the truth out of him tonight, she thought. Her lips curved up impishly. How could he resist confiding in a tie-snipping, paper-eating seductress? He'd do anything to keep her from embarrassing him in a posh restaurant, including confessing to his criminal activities, she thought with customary confidence. Wouldn't he?

CHAPTER FOUR

"What expensive restaurant are you taking me to?" Sara asked.

Her eyes raked speculatively over his casual attire. His "Texas tuxedo"—snug blue jeans and pale blue cambric shirt—clashed with her feminine off-the-shoulder white sundress.

A wide, appreciative grin slashed his long, lean face. "The most exclusive restaurant on the bay. Guess I should have told you not to wear anything frilly. Why don't you change into something more comfortable?"

"That's supposed to be *my* suggestion," Sara said teasingly. "Why don't you pour yourself a drink and I'll . . ." The intense look in his dark eyes kept her from completing the sentence. They slowly followed the elasticized band of lace from shoulder to shoulder. The shadow of cleavage barely exposed lured him inches closer.

"Need any help undressing?" Ryan whispered, his hands rising to rest lightly on the curve of her hips.

"No zipper. No buttons." Sara revealed the information without thinking. "One tug, and it's off."

Ryan kicked the front door shut with one foot. Alone, closed in the sanctity of her apartment, Sara raised her hand to the thick hair above the open collar of his shirt. Even though she wore spiky high heels, the top of her head barely reached his shoulders. Her head tipped back, she issued a silent invitation to be kissed. His dark head lowered fractionally; his hands moved to circle her waist. Her eyes drifted shut with a slight flutter.

"You'd better change in the other room," he suggested in a valiant effort to stem the flow of blood from his head downward.

"Mmmmmmm . . ." Sara kept her eyes closed and shook her loose curls from side to side. He was the kind of man who needed encouragement, she mused, her lips pursed in a half smile.

Ryan struggled silently. Lordy, lordy, he wanted to kiss her. But her blunt revelation about the precarious delicacy of her clothing left him knowing his curiosity about Sara, and about himself, couldn't be denied once he had folded her into his arms.

With a swift squeeze on her waist he stepped back. "I see you dug the Scotch out from between the sticky sweet liqueurs."

"Help yourself," Sara said. Nothing could be more humiliating than being puckered up and having a man politely excuse himself to get a drink, she thought, doing a low simmer.

The Scotch seemingly absorbed his attention, but covertly, through his lowered dark lashes, he watched Sara smooth her hands down the sides of her dress. His own personal cross to bear weighed heavily beneath his belt.

"Sara, I want you. My hands are perspiring from the need to touch you, but . . ." He raised his shoulders, then quickly let them slump. "There are things you don't know about me. I'm not certain you'll want to have anything to do with me once you know."

He's going to confess, Sara thought, her eyes widening with expectation.

"Yes?" she prompted.

Ryan tipped the amber liquid against his mouth, hoping it would give him courage. The booze didn't loosen his tongue. The problem lodged deep in his gut, refusing to free itself.

"Later. After dinner, when we're both relaxed, I'll explain," he said, procrastinating.

"Promise? There isn't anything too awful you can't tell me."

"You must have secrets of your own you've bottled up to be so understanding," Ryan said to postpone disclosure of his personal problem. Perhaps she would divulge her money problems once she realized he would do everything within his power to protect her.

"Are you teasing me about my weight again?" she asked, walking toward her bedroom to

71

change clothes. "I've adjusted to being smooth curves rather than straight lines."

Her inverted heart-shaped bottom swung enticingly, mesmerizing his appreciative eyes with their provocative jiggle. Before she closed the door, she winked with devilish glee.

Sara whipped the dress along with the half-slip over her head. After quickly shedding her shoes and pantyhose and throwing them in careless array on her bed, she crossed to the closet and pulled out the feminine version of the Texas tuxedo: faded jeans, pink and blue plaid western shirt, and tennis shoes. Boots were too hot for summertime wear.

Confident that Ryan planned to explain his involvement in the banking rip-off, Sara quietly rehearsed her response. She considered feigning shock but discarded the reaction. He needed a warm, supportive response. She'd let the deep concern be easily deciphered on her face.

Sara pulled the jeans up over her hips, then lay down on the bed to facilitate jerking the zipper up. Jeans on a woman weren't a perfect fit unless they appeared to have been painted on with a denim brush.

While she brushed her unruly blond locks back into some semblance of order, she schooled her face to appear genuinely concerned.

Lousy, she decided, dissatisfied with the smile that refused to droop.

With a final swipe of the brush through her hair, she gave up hopes of looking dejected. How could she force herself to be unhappy with

Ryan in the other room? He had said he wanted her, hadn't he? Although at the moment he held her she relished the thought of kissing him, her thoughts hadn't included the bedroom.

Others considered her ideas about sex prim, but Sara believed in love. "Romantic hogwash," one amorous male had declared, and Sara had argued that a man and woman sharing the epitome of intimacies should be more than handshaking acquaintances. With a laugh she had staunchly defended her belief: Mature men wanted friendship, the exchanging of confidences, trust, before—not after—sex.

What confounded Sara was that two proponents of casual sex had immediately proposed marriage, making her wonder what did the "modern man" want? An old-fashioned girl with an opposite viewpoint on physical intimacies? The only answer Sara had arrived at was that men, by and large, were complex creatures.

Ryan Crosby headed her list of contradictory men. He wanted her, yet he pushed her away. He wanted her to know the man prior to her *knowing* the male.

Sara pulled one stiff-jeaned leg across the other and poked her foot into her canvas shoe. She reversed the procedure and put on the other shoe. The second her clad foot touched the carpet she heard Ryan yell, "Isn't it supposed to take less time to change clothes than it is to start from scratch?"

"Impatient?" she shouted through the door.

"I'm hungry, aren't you?"

Surprisingly Sara wasn't. "I'll be right out."

"Ready?" Ryan asked, his eyes following the path of her voluptuous curves when she reentered the living room.

He wondered why the majority of men considered skinny women attractive. Nothing could be more feminine than the soft, lush lines of Sara's womanly body. From the front and the back viewpoints, no one but a blind man would have mistaken her for a man.

"Wait a sec."

Sara rushed into the kitchen and restocked her purse. *Who knows?* she rationalized out of habit, they might get stuck in a traffic jam, and Ryan would appreciate a little snack on the long drive to wherever they were eating.

"Why are you stuffing a soft pretzel into your purse?"

"Emergency rations," Sara explained. "You don't think I maintain this gorgeous figure without calorie intake, do you?"

Ryan shook his head in disbelief. "By all means, don't take any chances on starvation."

"I won't," she replied firmly. "Better to have and not eat than to want to eat and not have."

Cocking his head to the side, he wasn't certain he understood the twisted saying.

Sara grinned. "If I have a hidden source, I may not want it, but if I don't have food stashed away, I get uncontrollable hunger pangs."

"Sounds logical when you explain it," he replied thoughtfully. "You're a bit young to be considered a Depression baby, aren't you?"

Openly laughing at his referral to people who hoarded food because of deprivation during the 1930s amused her. Was he one of those people who believed society demanded a skin-and-bones physique? Others had tried to convert her to their strenuous ways of life and had failed.

"You a jogger?" she asked, observing the way the supple denim clung to his upper thigh muscles.

He chuckled and responded negatively.

"Biker?"

"No."

"Nautilus fan?"

"No." His grin widened into a full-fledged smile.

"Swimmer?"

"No."

Sara headed toward the front door. "You *must* exercise."

"Why?" he asked, close on her heels.

Her feet and her train of thought stopped suddenly. Ryan bumped into her backside before she could answer his question. With a perplexed expression on her face she looked over her shoulder and up at him. "I can't believe *I'm* suggesting a rigorous physical exercise program."

Ryan sidestepped Sara and opened the front door. "I can't either. But then you have a knack for doing the direct opposite of my expectations, haven't you?"

Curls bounced as she giggled at the absurd things she had done; she amiably agreed. He laced narrow fingers between hers. "Life isn't boring when Sara Hawkins is around. But I did try to be circumspect today." She shrugged and rubbed her palm over his. "All weekend I pep talked myself into cleaning up my act."

"Give it up as a lost cause, Sara. You aren't going to change; I wouldn't want you to."

"You wouldn't?" Sara asked, surprised. Everyone wanted her to suppress her inclination to do the absurd.

He feathered a butterfly kiss on the crown of her head rather than answer. Now was not the time to discuss the major flaw in her character. Perhaps her impulsive, compulsive behavior patterns matched up with the personality profile of a kleptomaniac. He didn't know, didn't want to let realities slip between them.

She touched the tender place in his heart he thought had hardened to the texture of cast iron. Somewhere in the last few months he'd forgotten how good it felt to smile, to laugh. She had changed that. Her humorous "I'll say anything that comes into my mouth, do anything that strikes me funny" behavior was infectious. He'd laughed at her antics, loving her dare-the-devil-himself attitude.

He helped Sara into his late-model Chevy as though she were a precious treasure. As he shut the door, her impish smile made his lips curve. Circling the car, he realized Sara wasn't the only one who had resolved to change her behavior radically. For hours he had sat, analyzing his morose attitudes. Growling and snarling had become ways of keeping women at a safe distance. He'd been deeply wounded, but he couldn't rationalize serving a lifetime sentence of misery as part of the healing process.

Sara cauterized the festering anger he felt with laughter. Jokingly he had told her he owed her. He did, and he prided himself on paying his debts in full.

"You haven't told me where we're going?" Sara reminded him once he had buckled his seat belt.

"My place." He saw her blond eyebrow arch toward the reckless curl on her forehead. "I'm going to wine, dine . . . and get to know all your deep, dark secrets."

Her hands smoothed over the tight cloth on her thighs. "I'm not secretive. I'm up front with everyone." *Not true, Sara.* She thought, rebuking herself. Her stomach still recoiled from the shoddy treatment of having digested the limb of a tree which had been processed into a sheet of paper.

With a flick of the key Ryan started the car, then pulled away from the curb. The guilty look on her face that Ryan observed confirmed his suspicions. Sara did have something to hide. How she had skillfully managed to delude the state's bank examiners, he didn't comprehend. Her blue eyes widened, rounded, with every prevarication she told.

"Nothing you'd like to undo or change?" he asked, probing gently.

"I wish I hadn't sent Elizabeth's résumé to

77

Jared McKnight," she replied, thinking of her latest prank. "But Elizabeth got even. She scared me to death when she called at the bank and told me she'd been hired."

"Sounds innocent to me," Ryan commented as he pulled off the access road onto the highway headed toward Galveston. "I'm certain your intentions were honorable."

"Not exactly. Jared advertised for a mistress." Sara waited for a scathing look or words of recrimination. Ryan kept smiling. "His sister placed the ad and substituted 'mistress' for 'social secretary.'"

"Sounds like something you'd do."

Sara paused, scooting sideways in her seat to get a full view of his strong profile without craning her neck. "I've done worse," she admitted.

"Such as?"

"Pulling the alarm in her father's jewelry store and pointing at Elizabeth when the police arrived. On second thought, the worst trick I pulled was when she dated a totally unsuitable rake."

Ryan's burst of laughter encouraged her to continue with the outlandish confessions.

"I knew Rake-the-Snake had a date with Elizabeth, so I positioned myself outside her door. When I saw him slithering down the corridor, I pretended to be knocking on the door. He introduced himself while his snake oil eyes stripped me of the conservative suit I wore." Her mobile face twisted with distaste. "The minute he called me darlin', I knew I was the instrument of poetic justice he was going to be clobbered with."

"Come on, Sara. Don't make me wait. What did you do to him?"

"I told him I worked for the Houston city welfare department, division of venereal disease control."

"You didn't!" Ryan exclaimed, laughing heartily. "Exit Mr. Rake-the-Snake?"

Giggling, Sara brushed the errant curl off her forehead. "I swear, he ran down the hallway with his legs crossed as though in fear it would fall off before he could get treatment."

"Must have been sleeping with your . . . friend."

"No. But he had big plans." Her blue eyes twinkled mischievously.

"Elizabeth didn't mind?"

"Well"—she paused—"not exactly. Not when I ripped my blouse, mussed my hair, and told her he'd gotten physical outside my door."

They laughed boisterously at the extent she had gone to give credence to the swift, just punishment she had doled out.

"You don't sound repentant," Ryan said mockingly.

"I did worry about Elizabeth's getting involved with Jared. I think I'm about to lose my best friend."

"Elizabeth is in love?"

Solemnly Sara nodded her head. "He mass produces jewelry; she designs individual pieces, but the professional conflict set aside, something tells me they're headed toward the altar. When Elizabeth refuses to tell me anything about the man she's dating, I know there is something going on."

"Is he about to get a visit from the VD control center?"

"Sara Hawkins never strikes twice in the same place. Besides"—she sighed with resignation—"Elizabeth has threatened me with bodily harm if I interfere."

Ryan reached across the console and lightly patted her knee, letting his hand linger, fingering the sharp crease in her jeans. "Maybe you'll find another friend to victimize," he said jokingly.

"Friends, real friends, are a limited commodity."

"Send me an application form. I'd like to send you a résumé." His voice, warm as his hands, sent sparks of electricity along her nerve endings. Her toes curled under as they received the tingling message.

Her imagination unfurling, Sara visualized a piece of sizzling red asbestos with a variety of personal questions. Requiring letters of recommendations might prove interesting. She scratched that idea. The last thing she wanted was a letter from an ex-girl friend verifying his assets.

Ryan turned off NASA 1 into the Bayfront Condominium complex. The tangy fragrance of salt water filtered into the car. Sara inhaled the heady smell.

"How wonderful to live near the water!" she exclaimed enthusiastically.

"My place is closer than *near*," he said, pointing to a thirty-foot sailboat. "It's *on*."

"You live on a boat?" She squealed with delight. "Like a swashbuckling pirate?"

A wicked, teasing gleam entered his dark eyes. "Want to see my gold earring?"

Sara leaned over and examined his earlobe. Sure enough, there was a tiny hole. Staid, No-Sense-of-Humor Crosby, disguised banking executive, was a bold, adventuresome pirate.

"When a man sails across the equator, he's entitled to wear an earbob. Unfortunately motorcycle gangs and druggies bastardized the custom," he explained.

While Ryan climbed out of the car and walked around to her side, Sara closed her eyes, relishing the image of Ryan facing the treacherous elements of nature. Windblown dark hair flying, courage stamped on his face, he fought hurricane-force gales. Sailing to the four corners of the earth, he hid gold coins on secret islands. He made maps with mysterious instructions. He—

"You have the most intriguing expression on your face," Ryan said.

"I'm a historical romance buff, so I was just imagining some heart-thumping scenarios," she explained as she climbed out of the car.

"Bodice rippers?" His dark eyes clung to her bountiful bosom. "I've read a few myself."

"You read romances?" she asked, aghast at his disclosure. The strong grip he had on her arm as

81

he walked her down the dock erased any qualms about a man reading romances.

"Put a sailing vessel on the cover, add a dash of adventure, a pinch of sensuality, and I'll buy it and read it cover to cover." The tiny lines webbed at the sides of his eyes deepened. "You're spunky enough to be a heroine. Shall I rip your shirt off now or later?"

Sara chuckled and took a quick survey to see if anyone was watching them. A cluster of teenagers sat on the far end of the wooden planks, fishing.

"Now," she replied in a chipper voice.

"You're confident I wouldn't dare, aren't you?" Two of his fingers defiantly hooked into the front of her shirt front.

Sara batted her eyelashes à la innocent damsel. "Have mercy," she begged prettily. "I'm destitute. Stranded in a foreign port without benefit of a male protector."

"I'm merciless. A savage of the seas," he growled. His free hand gestured toward the cabin. "Get below, wench. You're a tender morsel, and I intend to have my fill of your luscious body."

Caught up in the leading role of their enactment, Sara pretended to swoon. Ryan caught her by the arms, stooped, and grunted as he strained to hoist her over his shoulder.

"You're supposed to be struggling, not me," he whispered in admonishment.

"Uh-huh. Keep lifting. I've admired you from afar. Loved you forever. I'm looking forward to the ravishment!" she said in a low tone. Her smile widened when she realized how close to the truth her answer had been.

Ryan laughed triumphantly and smacked her on the rear. "We must have read different books."

He fully intended to set her on her feet, maybe give her a playful kiss, and pass the evening companionably, but the rounded curve of her derriere, the sweet pressure of her breasts against his upper back sidetracked his intent.

Sara's head spun dizzily as blood rushed to the roots of her blond hair. The hand that had slapped her soothed the stinging area by rubbing, massaging, gently stroking. Her eyes shut, she wished Ryan were a pirate and she the willing damsel.

The muscles of his back flexed against her tautening nipples. She reveled in the thought of having him carry her to their passionate destination. Certain the fantasy had ended when she felt herself being lowered from his shoulder, she squeezed her eyes shut tighter. Her fingers gripped his forearms.

"Sara, sweet Sara," Ryan whispered, his hands framing her face. "Do you fear ravishment?"

She sighed when he lightly kissed the corners of her mouth, the sensitive flesh along the curve of her jaw, the pulse rapidly beating at the base of her throat. She heard the snaps of her western shirt pulled apart, then felt the soft fabric slide down her shoulders. He tossed it aside; his eyes wondered over her flesh. One leg bent upward when his hand trailed slowly over her breast, waist, and hip.

Lazily her eyes opened. "I'm fearless."

Ryan leaned over her, an expression of intense concentration on his tanned features. She unbuttoned his shirt and tugged it loose from his waistband.

He shook his head as though forcing himself to wake from a beautiful dream. Her hands caressed his chest, sending shivers along his spine. His blood pounded as she barely rolled the nubble of his dark nipple between her thumb and forefinger, driving him close to the brink of losing his self-control.

His large hands cupped the underside of each breast; his thumbs worried the turgid tips. His mouth watered. He wanted to taste this firebrand, who tempted him as no woman had been able to for months and months. He heard the soft, seductive whisper of breath coming from her parted lips.

Kisses, light petting, no further, he thought. But the warning was cast aside like the salt spray in a high wind as he lowered them both onto the cabin's wide bed. He captured the inner moisture of her breath as he closed his lips over hers. The memory of Sara's sweet taste drove the tip of his tongue inside her. Sara bit the tip as though punishing him for making her wait, then massaged it with gentle, suckling sips.

Her womanly, lush breasts demanded attention as Sara arched her back toward him. The flimsy barrier of cloth was removed. Ryan heard enticing sounds from the back of her throat when he blindly explored the beaded tips with his sensitive fingers.

He emitted a low, tense groan when she twisted her hips, nuzzling the cradle of his hips. Captured in the strong currents of passion, he kissed a hot, moist path to the peak of first one breast, then the other.

Sara circled the sensitive pads of her fingertips over the muscles in his back. She didn't kid herself into believing she was being ravished by a bold pirate. Fully cognizant of who she was, where she was, and with whom, she felt a fiery yearning in the pit of her stomach no man had ever aroused.

Although he spoke not a word, his need swirled around her with the magnitude of a giant whirlpool. She could voice resistance but didn't. She could struggle against being sucked into the vortex of his powerful need but didn't. She wanted Ryan Crosby every bit as badly as he wanted her. She feared only that he would pull away, would stop before she had plummeted to the fathom-deep depths of his dark eyes.

As though he read her thoughts, Ryan made one last-ditch effort to get the situation back under control. He braced himself on his elbows, reached behind his waist, caught her hands, brought them over her head, then pulled a long draft of air into his lungs.

"Sara, what we're doing is wonderful, but—"

"But?" she interrupted. "Your parents must be traffic lights. You switch from green to red with only a few seconds' notice. I'm going to do the same thing to you that I do when I see a yellow light: put my foot on the accelerator."

The loose hold he had on her wrist was easily broken. Her fingers unbuckled his belt within seconds.

"Mr. Pirate-Banker, you are about to be robbed, raped, and pillaged. Don't fight me," she warned him, shoving his body flat on the bed while he suffered from shock. "I'll get my trusty rapier and draw and quarter you for beginners. Then I'll keelhaul each of the four pieces against the barnacles of your own ship. Anything left will be strung from the topsail. Got the picture?"

While she issued her dire threat, she slapped at the hands halfheartedly trying to keep his breeches in place. Ryan managed to get a death grip on the band of his Jockey shorts and refused to release them.

Frustrated by his lack of cooperation, Sara doubled over him and sank her teeth into the fleshy part of his hand.

"Yeee-ouch," Ryan bellowed. No longer playing, he grabbed her and flipped her over on her back. "You are the damnedest female I've ever met!"

CHAPTER FIVE

Anger quickly followed in the footsteps of frustration and hurt. "What about you? You're the only man in the entire universe who hangs on to his Jockey shorts as though saving himself for marriage."

"How do you expect me to react? That's the second time you've tried to shuck off my underwear!"

Her mouth short-circuited and bypassed her brain. "Are you gay?"

Ryan recoiled. "What made you ask that?" he demanded between clenched teeth.

"I don't know," Sara muttered truthfully. "Get off me. You weigh a ton. Where's my shirt, my purse?"

Ryan picked up her shirt and bra from the floor and tossed them to her. "Forget about gathering up your purse and hightailing it out of here." He shifted his weight to her side but kept one leg sprawled over her upper thighs. With one hand he helped her as she struggled into her bra, and then he drew her shirt closed as he randomly pushed together two of the snaps. "Why, Sara? Why that question?"

"I told you . . . I don't know. The word popped out of my mouth before I could stop it." The pained expression on his face, his considerate attempt to cover her nakedness diminished her anger. Had she taken a shot in the dark and landed on target? Was that the problem he had referred to earlier? She sure knew how to pick 'em, she thought in self-derision.

"To answer your blunt question, I'm not, nor have I ever been, involved with a man."

"I apologize for hitting below the belt," Sara muttered contritely. "No pun intended."

"Apology accepted."

"Can I have my purse now, please?" she politely asked.

"You are *not* leaving here until we've talked this out." Ryan clasped her hands over her head and refused to let her budge.

His lean, aroused body pressed her deeper into the mattress. The protective instinct to lambaste him ebbed further when she saw the bitter twist of his lips. They were back to square one: a ghoulish resemblance of a smile.

"My brain functions at its best when my mouth is stuffed with food. Good manners keep me from talking with my mouth full," she babbled. "Hand me my purse, and I'll share the pretzel with you."

His sharp laugh made her cringe. Intuition told her to cover her ears. She wasn't going to like what she was about to hear.

"I'll feed you when I've finished what we started," he replied in a dead tone. "Do you remember my being engaged when I first transferred to the Houston branch of the People's Bank?"

"Ryan, please, forget my wisecrack."

He shook his dark head, refusing to be sidetracked. "Susan was the most physically beautiful woman I'd ever met. Slender, auburn waistlong hair, legs that seemed to go on forever. She modeled for Neiman-Marcus fashion shows. I couldn't believe she accepted a date with me, much less agreed to get married a month later."

"I don't want to hear about your previous love life," Sara protested. Hearing the name of the woman he must have loved to distraction hurt equally as much as his rejection of her own less than perfect body. "I'm not going to listen."

She closed her eyes as though doing so affected her hearing.

"You will listen. You will hear. And you will understand why I stopped making love to you."

The hell I will. Her eyes flashed. Her lips clamping tighter than her eyelids, she began humming loudly.

"Stop it, Sara. Dammit! I didn't carry you down here with some perverted idea of making you want me, then refusing at the last minute."

One blue eye opened, expressing her skepticism. The tuneless hum droned louder. He couldn't make her listen if she didn't want to.

"I can shout louder than you can hum," Ryan yelled. "Susan jilted me!"

The humming abruptly stopped. Sara couldn't believe what she had heard. No woman in her right mind would jilt Ryan Crosby.

Jilted you? she mouthed soundlessly. Sympathy didn't erase her frustration or hurt. Other men, and for that matter, women had broken off engagements at a moment's notice and recovered. He didn't have a monopoly on misery. Regaining a fraction of her usual voice, she whispered, "For months you barked at me like a junkyard dog because some—some—cutesy-butt walked out on you?"

Ryan released his grip on her wrists, moved to the edge of the bed, and sat up, his back toward her. A tearing sensation from deep in his gut ripped his secret loose. "Susan jilted me on our wedding day."

"Why?"

He shrugged. "I don't know. Ten minutes before the ceremony she called the minister and had the message relayed to me. Can you imagine how I felt? There must be something drastically wrong with me. A woman wouldn't walk away without explanation unless there were."

"And you haven't . . ." she muttered, realizing the disastrous effect his fiancée's act had had on his male ego. It was unforgivable to make him wait nervously at the church and then not show up. Ryan was the one who had had to face the disbelieving looks, answer humiliating questions, accept the pity or sympathy of friends and relatives, and return the stacks of gifts. No wonder he hadn't dated or become involved again.

"No. I haven't. Haven't wanted to. Haven't been certain I could until you pounded on my heart with your fist." His face averted, his hands gripping the edge of the bed, Ryan waited for a scathing comment or brittle laughter.

Barely moving, Sara linked her small finger with his. She had to say something, do something, but her tongue seemed paralyzed. In every situation there had to be a positive side. There had to be something good coming from bad. But what?

"Ryan, you have to realize she did what she had to do. Breaking the engagement wasn't a reflection on you as a man."

He snorted, indicating his doubt. "Gelding without anesthetic would have been kinder."

"Don't say that," Sara said protestingly as she sat up and looped her arm across his stooped shoulder. "You should have thanked your lucky stars you escaped an unhappy marriage and gone on living without looking back."

"Oh, Sara," he murmured, dejected, "that's like telling you to quit eating."

"Exactly! When I let other people influence me with what they thought I should look like, I made myself miserable."

"You're equating sex with eating?" he queried, his head shaking at her convoluted logic.

"Aren't they both primary human drives? In fact, man craves food long before he needs sex." Sara placed her hand on his jaw and turned his head toward her. With the only source of light coming from the porthole, the cabin held little light. "Listen to me; listen closely because I'm telling you something I've never told anyone."

Ryan twisted his torso toward her but had difficulty looking her in the eyes.

"By the time I turned fourteen I knew boys preferred cutesy-butts. 'Get the fat off,' I told myself. And I tried. Have you any idea how many bizarre diets there are? Could you live on hard-boiled eggs and grapefruit? Or drink water instead of eating? Or have a needle stabbed into your rear end once a day?"

He shook his head in response to her string of questions.

"I swear, my calorie intake soars simply by my reading *Gourmet* magazine! Anyway, by the time I was sixteen I was absolutely neurotic. My happiness hinged on seeing the magic numbers one-zero-zero appear when I weighed in every morning. I was a prime candidate for the illness Karen Carpenter died from, believe me."

She took a deep breath, organizing her thoughts. "Then, without any specific thing influencing my life, I decided there had to be something better in life than pinching an inch. I decided that what's inside my head, what I think of myself, are more important than having a man leer at me. And you know what?"

She didn't wait for a response but rushed on. "I like Sara Hawkins. Better yet, since I've worked at being beautiful on the inside, other people have told me I'm beautiful inside *and out.* It's how you perceive yourself, not how you think others see you, that matters. It's how *you* feel about making love to a woman that's important."

"But what if I can't—"

"You can worry yourself to death with what ifs. What if the boat had exploded before we undressed? What if the green people from Mars invade earth? What if, what if, what if!" She paused and inhaled deeply. "What if you and I made love and it turned out to be the most breathtaking experience you'd had in your life?"

"What if it weren't?" Ryan asked, verbalizing the opposite possibility.

"Then we'd try, try again," she answered with a cheeky grin. "We won't give up until we get it right."

"You're willing to risk it, knowing what you know? Knowing I wasn't man enough to hang on to my fiancée?"

"It was Susan's problem—not yours. She wasn't woman enough to keep you. I'm willing to risk making love with you regardless of fears, either mine or yours."

"Do you want to eat dinner first?"

Sara snuggled up to him and felt the tension across his shoulder blades. "Your lips are delicious, but for once, I'm not going to latch onto them like a piece of fresh strawberry shortcake. Nor am I going to make wild threats to get you to take your clothing off. I care for you, Ryan Crosby."

Slowly Ryan lowered her shoulders to the pillow. He hadn't heard or thought of the word "care" in a long, long time. As he brushed his lips lightly across her love-swollen mouth, his eyes closed, and he realized that he too cared. Selfish desire to prove himself as a man was set aside. He wanted to love Sara Hawkins, intimately, because the golden glow surrounding her made him warm . . . happy. And he hadn't been contented with himself in months.

Concerned about his vulnerability, Sara sweetly returned his kiss. She understood the stumbling block, the reason behind his negative attitude, his lack of self-worth. Her fingers threaded themselves through the dark hair at his nape to the crown of his head. His mouth closed over hers and deepened the kiss. She could almost hear his thoughts. With each probe, each swirl, he told her of his rising ardor.

With the greatest care, he removed first her clothing, then his own. What could have been awkward was beautiful. Her lush hourglass figure intrigued him. His lips and hands, a contrast of moistness and dryness, openly caressed each feminine mound and curve with unsurpassed gentleness. He cared, and he showed her how much with each loving stroke.

"My lovely Sara," he whispered, moving over her, "you've taught me to smile. Now guide me, teach me to love."

A spray of goose bumps spread above her breasts, her back arched as she curled her fingers around him and led him into her welcoming femininity. For long moments he held both of them perfectly still, suspended in time and motion.

"I'd almost forgotten . . ." he murmured.

With each long, sure stroke, his confidence built. He felt her hips circle, beckoning him to climb quickly to the heights of rapture, but he held back. He wiped the painful memories aside as carefully as he removed the beads of salty dampness above her lips with the tip of his tongue. This blissful feeling couldn't last forever, but he fervently wished it could.

The urgent expression on her face, the tight hold of her fingers on the flesh of his hips signaled him not to wait. With the heel of his hand nestled against her warmth, he parried each powerful thrust of her hips.

Her blue eyes glazed with pleasure, Sara smiled. Ryan had forgotten nothing. He knew, better than any man, how to take her aggressively past the boundaries of mundane lovemaking. He wanted fulfillment for both of them.

A tingling sensation traveled from her heels up to the calves of both legs, then journeyed to the nerve endings in her scalp. With her eyes squeezed shut by the glorious sensation, with her legs gripping his hips, with her buttocks clenched, Sara's mind blew apart with his final thrust.

Ryan sucked in air to keep from shouting her name. But in his mind a permanent imprint boldly branded it on his heart. All other names and faces faded into black infinity. The shackles binding him with fears of his sexual adequacy shattered. Only the pure glow of Sara Hawkins burned deep within him.

A gurgle of triumphant, joyous laughter bubbled in her throat as he thanked her in a way they both understood. Between them there were no ifs, only the satiated release from fear and doubt.

Heat, intense heat, radiated from Ryan's face. Sara framed the side of his face with her small hand. A dark fire burned from the depths of his eyes. His lips, curved up, gently closed over her own.

Drawing back, shifting his weight beside her, he whispered, "I touched the beauty within you, and it made me whole. I'm a new man."

A sassy quip darted behind her lips, but Sara raked the tip of her tongue over the roof of her mouth to remove it. Her smile rivaled the secretive upsweep of the lips of the Mona Lisa. "I'm glad . . . for both of us."

Ryan sniffed the air. "Do you smell something peculiar?"

Before Sara had time to react, he rolled to his feet and bounded out of the small room. A whiff of bluish smoke identified the odor.

"Oh, my God," she murmured as she yanked the sheet off the bed, speedily draped it around herself yoga fashion, and followed him. "The boat's on fire!"

Sara rushed into the galley, halted, and burst into fits of laughter at what she saw. Ryan stood, stark naked, holding the charred remains of a casserole between two thick potholders. The

96

woebegone expression on his face made each burst of laughter harder, louder.

"This is your dinner you're laughing at," he told her. "I put it in the oven before I went to pick you up." His drooping lips turned in the opposite direction. "When you get control of yourself, go get a pair of shorts out of the dresser for me and your purse."

Eyes dancing with mirth, Sara saucily said, "Wouldn't you rather have me whip up an omelet while you get dressed?"

"Out, woman. Keep shimmying around in that bedsheet, and you can forget about dinner," he laughingly commanded.

"I wouldn't mind . . ."

"Don't say it. I'm master of this ship and master of your fate," he said with piratelike bravado.

"The wench does the cooking, Oh-Great-Thief-of-the-Seas," she glibly retorted.

"My ship, my rules." He set the blackened dish on the stove top and dismissed her by turning to the half-size refrigerator, which he bent at the waist to open.

Sara covered her mouth to hide a giggle but couldn't refrain from commenting, "You have a magnificent tush."

She heard Ryan chuckle as he wiggled from the hips down. "You really don't have a filter between your brain and your mouth, do you?"

"You're standing there buck naked, scrounging in the icebox, and you call me uninhibited?" Sara gave a lusty, deep-throated chuckle.

"You're wicked, woman. And I love it. Now scoot! See if you can get dressed in less than five minutes."

"I have to get dressed?" Sara protested.

"Unless you want to parade naked on the deck, I think it would be a good idea," he answered, chuckling at the thought of the shocked expression on the faces of the people in the nearby condos if they saw two respectable bankers romping around in their birthday suits. "My neighbors are clients of the bank. You wouldn't want a run on the bank tomorrow, would you?"

"I'm certain I could dream up some lucid explanation."

Ryan laughed aloud. "I'm sure you could."

For the first time since she had entered the ship, Sara took note of her surroundings as she proceeded back to the bedroom. Everything was compact and orderly. To her right were storage cabinets; to her left were two doorways. Unable to resist, she opened the first door and found a small bedroom with bunk beds decorated with blue nautical coverlets that matched the miniature curtains over the porthole.

The second door opened into a small bathroom. All the facilities were there but were scaled down to fit the size of the ship. Everything had a place, and everything was in place. Typical, she thought remembering his fetish for neatness, but she also realized that clutter in these small quarters would drive a person crazy.

"Quit poking around. I need your help," she

heard Ryan shout. "Come up on deck when you're ready."

"Yes, my captain," she yelled back over her shoulder. "Jeez, you're bossy."

Deep male laughter followed her down the corridor. "You've finally admitted something you should have realized months ago."

"What's that?"

"I *am* your boss!"

The note of glee in his voice stroked her rather than rubbed her the wrong way. Male assertion, pride in himself, coated with globs of humor, made Ryan Crosby an appetizing dish.

The mussed bed, the erotic smell of their love-making lingering in the air, made her knees weak as she picked up her clothes from the floor of the captain's bedroom and began dressing. Just allowing herself to breathe in the essence of the man made a flush spread over her body.

Feeling good about herself, about Ryan, she put two fingers to her lips and blew a kiss into the bedroom before she closed the door and headed toward the top deck.

Twilight, the edge of darkness, greeted Sara as she stepped outside. A wide grin on his face, Ryan gestured toward the floor of the deck to her purse. "Hope you didn't mind my opening it. Appetizers are served."

"Emergency rations," Sara stated, her voice brimming with good-natured fun. On the small aft table a paper plate with half a soft pretzel sat next to a bowl of salad. "Next time you won't scoff when I prepare to leave my apartment."

"You'll have to pardon my nibbling before you arrived. My half of the pretzel saved me from starvation." His eyes slowly enveloped her from her disarrayed blond curls to the painted tips of her bare toes. "You're gorgeous."

A bit shy from his compliments, Sara tossed the blue jean cutoffs to him. Saved by her quick tongue, she said, "I thought you were out here naked as a blue jay, and I didn't want the women to miss out on a rare treat."

Ryan snapped the waistband of his swim trunks. "Their disappointment is acute. I heard all the women hanging over the edges of their balconies heave a sigh when I covered up."

"You're awfully conceited, Captain," Sara said teasingly as she picked up her share of the pretzel and moved to his side. "One night does not a king make!"

The barbless quip held a challenge he couldn't resist. Not answering but taking her hand, he drew it to his lips and peppered love bites from the pads on her fingers to the sensitive skin at her wrist. Laughter beamed from his eyes when he stroked her love line with the tip of his tongue. Her eyelids had lowered. Her thumb caressed the side of his jaw. The flickering flames of barely concealed desire brought her closer.

"King Ryan, I presume?" she huskily inquired.

Determined to let her have a taste of her own humor, he watched her eyes close, reached behind himself, and picked up a piece of the crab bait.

"You're under my power?"

Sara nodded. "Your wish is my command, Sire."

"Catch dinner," he crooned as he slapped the crab bait, a cold, clammy chicken wing into the palm he'd just kissed.

Jumping back, squealing at the same time, Sara threw the bait and the attached string on the deck. "What is that?"

"Chicken wing. It's what we're going to use to catch dinner," he answered, laughing, slapping his knee at her squeamishness.

"Dirty trick! Here I was, getting hot and bothered, and what do you do?"

"Pay you back for your smart remark. Now pick up your bait, and watch," he instructed. His dark eyebrow raised, he added, "This is your first lesson in patience. I expect you to learn from this."

"A bad habit is what patience is. Synonymous with dithering, indecisiveness," she said playfully. "Impatience and impetuosity are virtuous."

Ryan sniffed derisively. The string, chicken wing attached, landed with a splash, but he held on to the knot at the end of the string.

"Hope you take a double serving of both virtues while I'm eating flaky morsels of crabmeat." He leaned on the back rail, his fingers attuned to what took place on the bottom of Clear Lake.

"Crabs live in tin cans, not the bottom of the bay," Sara said banteringly. "Next you'll be telling me fish don't grow in fish markets."

"Shame on you. Are you telling me you've never eaten crabs or fresh fish when you live on the Gulf of Mexico?" He didn't know whether or not she was teasing him. In typical Sara fashion she could be hustling him. "I won't swallow that bit of fabrication, Sara Hawkins."

"Would you believe my dad owns a fleet of shrimp boats and I used to spend my summers as a deck hand?"

"Nice try, but I read your personnel file."

"Okay, how about this?" Her imagination began running wild.

"While you're thinking up some totally outrageous story, drop your line over the side."

She complied automatically. Every good whopper based itself on an element of truth. "When you kissed me, did you notice anything?"

Grinning, Ryan boldly answered, "I noticed the tips of your breasts instantly become as hard as pearls. Little moans of pleasure come from low in your throat. You tend to nuzzle with your hips instead of your nose. Other than that, I didn't notice a thing."

Distracted by his recitation, Sara almost lost her train of thought.

"You were saying?" Ryan prompted, smiling benignly.

Bemused, Sara couldn't get her thoughts straight. "Oh, yeah. Where was I?"

"About to tell a windy story."

"Salt . . . you taste salt when you kiss me, don't you?"

"Honey, sweet, luscious honey," he whispered. Standing, their elbows touching, her face turned up to his, he remembered the taste and licked his lips.

Sara groaned. "You're not making telling this story easy. Keep your tongue in your mouth where it belongs, and teach me patience. It's definitely in short supply where I'm standing."

The husky laugh she had learned to love, accompanied by a heartbreaking smile, made her completely miss the sharp tugs on the string in her hand.

"You've got one!"

"But I'd like another," she replied, her mind belowdeck.

"Sara, slowly lift the bait up."

"I'd rather skip the snack and get right to the main meal," she muttered but followed his directions.

"Let him get a good hold."

"My thoughts exactly," she replied, dropping her eyes to the jerking string. Inch by inch she raised the bait until a plate-size crab dangled between the water and the boat.

"Don't rush. He'll let go!" He adroitly tied his line to the railing.

"So I've been told," she said cheekily. Concentrating on the free claw waving in her direction in an intimidating manner, she considered

103

dropping it back into the bay. "Ryan! Ryan! Don't leave me now!"

"Slowly . . . slowly," he said encouragingly, scooting an ice chest behind her.

"Jeez, it's going to be a contest to see who eats whom!"

"Throw it back," he ordered abruptly.

"No way. Dinner's on the string. We're going to eat this baby!"

Ryan reached across her and shook the line. The crab plunked back into the water.

"You rat! My dinner is on the bottom of the bay, crawling around again! That was cruel," she said. "My one and only catch, and you ruined it!"

"Did you see the stuff that looked like moss on the underside?"

"Yes, but we could have scraped off the seaweed."

"Wasn't seaweed. It was a mother crab with eggs attached. It's illegal to keep them."

"Illegal?"

Ryan pinched her cheek lightly to dispel the look of frustration from her face. "No little crabs next year if you catch the mamas." A frown crossed his face. "Sara, I didn't—"

"I follow the motto printed on money: In God we trust; everybody else needs protection," she interrupted lightheartedly. "Don't worry. I always take responsibility for everything I do."

"You're one in a million," he said softly.

"That's what I tell everyone. One slightly plump Sara Hawkins is better than a million—"

Ryan smothered her wisecrack with a sharp

104

kiss. Never again, he vowed, would he let Sara hide her emotions behind a smart remark. The silent promise reminded him of one he'd made earlier. Mentally he canceled the earlier vow. She could steal every dime in the bank, plus the furnishings, and he'd cover for her.

The sobering thought ended the kiss. "Let's try again."

"For another crab, the kiss, or the cabin below," Sara answered, giving him a wide range of choice. She glanced at the string tied to the rail.

To Ryan her last phrase was the only one he heard. He held Sara close as he turned, untied the string, and let the splash of water answer her question.

CHAPTER SIX

Ryan leaned back in his chair and allowed his eyes to seek and find what his mind had been mulling over all morning: Sara Hawkins. The previous evening they had laughed about a run on the bank. This morning, with long lines in front of each teller's window, the bank had the appearance of a run, but in actuality it was a typical middle-of-the-month summer day. Customers withdrew money for traveler's checks, and deposited checks to cover the checks they had written the previous weekend.

Nothing has changed, he mused, *except me.* Long after midnight, after he had taken Sara home, he had lain awake, listening to the early-morning tide gently splash against the boat, smelling the heady mixture of salt air and the light fragrance of lilac she wore that clung to the sheets of his bed. He'd found himself smiling, chuckling over the wild tales she had spun, given the least provocation. He'd heard half a dozen different stories about who her parents were and how she had been reared, one story more preposterous than the next. Finally, she had confessed, tongue in cheek, that her father owned the chain of banks they both worked for. Ryan's sides had ached from laughing. He hadn't enjoyed the company of a woman in months, and Sara seemed to make up for what he had lacked.

Uninhibited, she had appeared to blossom with each burst of laughter. *Charisma*, he thought, finding a single descriptive word to explain the elusive personal quality that set her apart from others, *and a positive self-image*, he added—traits he had set aside in favor of wallowing in the empty shell of self-doubt and self-pity. But she had thumped against his heart literally and figuratively.

Now simply watching her smile and greet each customer made the blood course through his veins. He wanted to test his memory to see if her lips could possibly be as delectable as he remembered. Absentmindedly his hand flipped through the stack of printout sheets on his desk. He'd much rather it followed the svelte curves of Sara's waist and hips or roamed at will through the halo of blond curls on her head.

Ryan shifted in his desk chair uncomfortably, a rush of passion building inside him. Unwilling to wait until the end of the workday, he quickly scribbled a note and rubber-banded it to a stack of money straps. After leaving the note with his secretary to be delivered to Sara, he headed toward the secluded bank vault.

Sara excused herself from waiting on her customer and grinned as she accepted the wrappers from Ryan's secretary. *What are these for?* she wondered, glancing at the neatly bound green bills in her cash drawer. She slipped the note out. What had she done wrong? She'd been too busy to get into trouble!

"Would you mind rushing?" the customer asked politely. "My boss is on a rampage. He told me to get those quarters immediately. In his book, 'immediately' means 'yesterday.'"

Caught between doing her job and wondering what the note contained, Sara placed the note in the cash drawer as she stooped beneath it to get a tray of quarters. She straightened. Her mind on the contents of the note, and not watching what she was doing, the edge of the tray caught the lip of the counter. Rolls of quarters spilled forward and rolled off the front.

"Grab 'em," she exclaimed.

Overbalancing the tray, she tilted the remaining rolls in her own direction. *Butterfingers!* she thought, berating herself. In what seemed to Sara like slow motion, the rolls fell off both edges before she could stop them. Orville Redenbacher's popcorn would have been put to shame compared to the effect of the rolls bursting open, bouncing, twirling, rolling among the feet of customers in the crowded lobby.

Squeals of shock and delight bubbled throughout the bank. Grown men and women stooped down to retrieve the quarters as though they were thousand-dollar bills.

On hands and knees one man began scooting

them into a large pile. "Hey, Sara," he said jokingly, "thanks for the free samples."

Her sense of humor never flagging, she shouted, "Check your shoes, the cuffs of your pants. Nobody leaves until every quarter is accounted for! Lady, I saw you put a handful down your front!"

Male laughter, interspersed with female giggles, gave the cool, staid atmosphere of the bank a face-lift. Shouts of "Here's one," "get that one," "there's one under your shoe, you devil," echoed off the marble walls.

The other tellers' heads poked over the counter. A cross between abject dismay and hidden exhilaration was clearly written on their faces. Sara shrugged and rolled her eyes heavenward.

"The person who gathers the most wins a lollipop," she yelled, encouraging the stragglers standing around to get in on the action.

"Banker's holiday! Sara's giving away candy to the sucker who gives the money back!"

Another burst of laughter increased the festive mood of the customers.

"How many did you drop?" one of the customers shouted.

"A hundred dollars' worth, four hundred quarters in all," she answered, "but some of them fell back here. Just pile them on the counter, and I'll run them through the counting machine later."

"Hey, look here," a woman shouted. "There's a whole roll wedged between those planters."

Two boys rushed from opposite sides of the lobby and grabbed for the roll at the same time. "Mine!" they each shouted, determination in their voices.

"Don't fight," Sara yelled. "I'll give both of you a lollipop."

When she saw the look of disappointment on the adults' faces, she added, "You all deserve a reward. Bring your quarters over here, and I'll kiss the men and give the women candy!"

"Sara!" Richard squeaked from the cage next to hers. "You can't kiss all those men."

"Sure I can!" Sara replied. "You don't think I'm going to miss an opportunity to show our customers what a friendly bank we are, do you?"

A line began forming in front of Sara's cage. The man who had asked for the quarters to begin with held out three rolls and a handful of quarters.

"Gosh, I really started something, didn't I?" he asked, his voice filled with glee.

"One of us did," Sara answered dryly, handing him a lollipop and a full tray of quarters. "Show me where you want your kiss."

His finger pointed toward his upswept lips, then moved over to his cheek. "I'm married," he explained.

"Don't worry. Your wife won't believe this when you tell her anyway," Sara cheekily replied, planting a chaste peck on his cheek. "Sorry for the delay. Hope you don't get in trouble with your boss."

Sara watched his eyes round as though

110

shocked. His finger began stabbing the air. When she turned around to see what he was pointing toward, her heart sank to her toes.

"Ryan, uh, uh," she stammered. How was she going to explain having a long line of customers, each with a fistful of quarters, waiting for either a kiss or a piece of candy?

Inwardly she groaned. He'd never believe what had happened.

"What's going on?" he asked at the same time a grinning man stepped to the counter, deposited coins from his hands, then reached into his jacket pockets to pull out more.

"Your kiss has to be sweeter than any commercially produced candy," the customer crooned suavely.

She watched Ryan's eyes as they swept over the quarter-strewn floor inside her cage like a wide broom. "It's your fault I dropped a tray of quarters," she stated. *A good offense is the best defense,* she thought.

"I'm ready, Sara. Don't let your grumpy boss giving you the evil eye inhibit you," the customer whispered in a loud stage voice.

"Reward," she explained, knowing Ryan wasn't in the least bit going to like her kissing the attractive man on the other side of her cage.

Sara stood on tiptoe, leaned over, and gave him a swift peck.

"You missed. A real kiss, or I keep the loot," he said teasingly, reaching into the cage and firmly gripping her shoulders. "Like this."

The tips of her toes raised off the floor. She felt

111

herself being hauled forward. She could taste the hint of laughter on the man's mouth. Evidently he planned on enjoying her predicament to the fullest.

"All right!" he shouted once he had set her down. "I'm banking here forever!"

Twin flags of red embarrassment flashed on her cheeks. Nervously she glanced over her shoulder. Ryan stoically leaned against the partition separating her cage from Richard.

"It didn't mean anything," she muttered in his direction.

She thanked her lucky stars that the next three people were women customers. The pile of coins grew rapidly. In a valiant effort to regain her aplomb, Sara passed out the lollipops. The two boys who had fought over the roll were next. Casting Ryan what she hoped was a triumphant glance, she directed her wobbly legs toward the swinging door into the lobby. There wasn't any way for her to lean far enough forward to kiss their cheeks.

"Don't slobber on me, lady," one boy protested as he crossed his arms in front of his face. "I don't even let my mother kiss me."

Laughing, Sara gave him several pieces of candy. "Come back in a few years," she said jokingly.

The younger boy lifted his cheek and held out his hand. "Dummy there don't know a good thing when he sees it."

When the fortune hunters, bounty in hand, had been rewarded, Sara ducked her head and

112

returned to her cage, her eyes glued to the empty floor. Ryan had picked up the money and placed it in stacks of ten dollars.

"Thanks," she said, tugging her shirttail back in her suit skirt. "Do you want to yell at me here or in your office?"

"Read the note," Ryan answered curtly. He strode away before she could explain precisely why she had dropped the tray of quarters to begin with.

Sara shrugged. He had never minded giving her a tongue-lashing in front of the other tellers on any other occasion, she thought, hoping it was a good sign. He had said he'd changed. Maybe he had. Maybe she'd been such a good influence on him he could ignore her little idiosyncrasics. Her eyes riveted on the mound of quarters, she shrugged again.

Read the note . . . read the note, echoed in her mind as she opened the folded sheet of paper. *"Urgent: Come to the cash vault. Bring your purse,"* she read.

My purse? In the cash vault? Oh, no, she moaned. *He told me he wouldn't take any more unless we . . .* Her imagination took a giant wild leap. He wanted her to be the bagman. She looked down at her satchel type of purse. He could stuff thousands of dollars into it, but what then? Pilfering small amounts and replacing them were one crime, but my God! Her whole body shuddered. Had he changed for the worse instead of the better? Was he willing to forgive the reward system she had doled out if she stashed stacks of money into her purse? Did he really think he could get away with this?

I'm no thief, she wanted to scream in loud protestation. Just because she cared about him didn't mean she was ready to be fitted out for a prison uniform.

Don't go, she instructed herself sternly. *Let him wait, suffer, think you're coming, but don't.*

Sara took the sign that read NEXT WINDOW PLEASE and raked the pile of quarters into a small burlap sack. The coins clinked together. The sack became heavier and heavier. Tears gathered at the corners of her eyes. She had to stop him. One way or another, she had to.

Ryan opened the heavy steel door on the pretext of getting reserve cash out for each of the tellers. Originally he had planned on secluding Sara in the confines of the vault and kissing her until they both were dizzy. But thanks to her outlandish form of retrieving the dropped quarters, she had received more kisses in ten minutes than he had given her altogether.

Unable to watch man after man kiss Sara, he had been reduced to groveling at her feet to get the rest of the coins. He chuckled to himself. The note must have unraveled her enough to make her careless with the tray of coins. Somehow the thought of Sara's being shaken up rather than being the one doing the shaking pleased him.

His eyes scanned the stacks of money. To most people, the piles represented houses, cars, groceries, paid bills, security, but to Ryan it could have been Monopoly money. It wasn't his. He merely kept track of it for other people.

"Sara," he muttered, "when are you going to learn to keep the denominations separated?"

The orderliness of the vault was her responsibility, not his. A couple of days ago he would have stormed back upstairs and demanded she straighten up the mess. Instead, he patiently removed the misplaced bundles and sorted them out on the floor. Doubting she had turned the bills all one way, he curled the money and slid it from between the stack and fanned the money out.

Sara quietly watched from the barely opened doorway. Appalled, she saw Ryan hunkered down, grinning as he pushed the money back into the strap, then busily removed more stacks of money and placed them on the floor. Sara asked loudly, "What are you doing?"

Ryan glanced up, saw the expression on her face, and roguishly decided to do a bit of truth bending himself. His dark brows wiggling, he answered, "Cleaning up. This messy money needs to be hauled out of here."

She stretched her arms straight out from her body and blocked the entrance to the vault. "You can't! You'll get caught and sent to Sing-Sing . . . or wherever they send bank robbers!"

"Bring your purse over here, and you can go with me," he said, cartwheeling a bundle of hundred-dollar bills in her direction.

Sara jumped back as though he had thrown a

115

stick of dynamite in her direction. "Have you gone crazy?"

"Crazy?" Ryan thoughtfully stroked his chin with one finger. He couldn't deny having been a mite crazy when he watched her kissing a long line of men. "Only where you're concerned."

"Put it back." Sara picked up the cash he had tossed, then bent over and grabbed up more piles of money. "I can't believe you think I'd be your bagman."

"Bagman?"

She looked around the nearly empty room. "Is there an echo in here? Bagman," she repeated. "You know, the person who stashes away the ill-gotten gains. Isn't that why you instructed me to bring my purse?"

Standing up, grinning wider, Ryan reached for her. "I had a craving for honey and soft pretzels," he crooned, his eyes filled with laughter.

"Your elevator doesn't reach the penthouse," she said scoffingly, pointing to her temple. "I know why you wanted me and my purse down here. It's disgusting! I wouldn't involve *you* in committing a crime. You think—"

He swiftly bent down and nibbled at her lower lip. "Honey." Distracting her with light flicks of his tongue, he removed her purse from her arm and flipped the catch open. "Pretzels?"

Befuddled, embarrassed by having jumped to the wrong conclusion, Sara stuttered, "J-j-jelly beans."

"I'll settle for honey."

Ryan hummed his lips against hers appreciatively. He heard her purse drop to the floor. One arm wrapped itself around his neck; the other, around his waist. His eyelids drifted shut when she cuddled closer. She swayed her hips provocatively against him, refusing to part her lips.

"You're dealing with a dangerous criminal," he told her. He pulled her closer, loving the feel of her breasts flattening against his chest. "I want you, Sara Hawkins. Right now, right here in front of all those dead Presidents immortalized on the front of those thousands of dollars."

"Isn't there something in the bank's policy book regarding necking in the money vault?" she asked tantalizingly.

"Under 'Restricted Area'?" His hand crept beneath her suit jacket toward the front.

"I'm certain it's forbidden." She sighed when his thumb and finger circled the tip. "Forbidden" lightly echoed in the silence. Nothing Ryan did with his sensitive hands should be forbidden, she mused. She played a game of cat and mouse with her hands, dodging from shoulder blade to shoulder blade, up and down his spine.

His lips grazed the side of her neck when her hands settled low on his hips. She tucked her fingers inside his back pockets as though magically having found a way to eliminate one layer of restrictive clothes. His buttocks tightened in response to the caress.

"You're tempting me far more than those

bundles of money," he rasped. His mouth nipped its way to the vee of her blouse.

The tiled floor beneath his feet would make a lousy substitute for a bed, he mused, keeping a tight rein on himself. But she felt so good rubbing against him. Could he be content with touching the soft swell of her breasts without being able to remove her bra? Inwardly he knew he couldn't.

One flat button slipped open without help. He took advantage of the unexpected gift by lightly running the tip of his tongue along the restraining lace. Two more buttons, and he'd be home free. Concentrating, he willed the inanimate objects to be subjugated to his train of thought. The buttonholes held stubbornly even when he nudged them with his chin.

In an awkward, stooped position, he turned Sara's back to the wall. He heard her aroused gasps and knew their voiceless meaning. Hips thrust against hers, there was no hiding the effect she had on him.

"Have you taken your lunch hour yet?" he murmured. "Or better yet, aren't you feeling good enough to work this afternoon? I think I'm coming down with some sort of debilitating attack."

"Yes, I've had lunch. No, I can't plead a migraine. Today's the fifteenth."

"Fifteenth?" he questioned.

"Of the month. Neither of us can leave early without half the employees' quitting by two o'clock."

118

"I heard a customer yell today is a banker's holiday. Let's celebrate," he said coaxingly. He sucked her lobe between his lips. "Let's christen the bank vault."

Sara shook her head halfheartedly. Her blue eyes glassy with the need he had provoked, she tried to clear her head of the desire to slump to the floor.

Ryan, his dark eyes shut, didn't see her nod, but he felt her lips stroking back and forth on his throat. He slipped her silk blouse out of the skirt waistband and stroked the full cup of her bra. Why didn't she wear one of those front-clasp things? He silently cursed.

The kneaded flesh beneath his hands sent messages of fiery delight through her. Instinctively one knee drew close to cross over the other. Her upper thigh touched him intimately.

"Touch me," he pleaded before he wetly kissed her.

She knew she shouldn't; she knew they both would leave the vault frustrated, but she couldn't deny either of them the pleasure. Her hand, at first tentative, became bold. As she stroked, he drove deeper and deeper into the hot cavern of her mouth. He inched her skirt upward until he could wedge his hand between her legs.

"Pantyhose," he moaned, begrudging the sheer nylon barrier its right to stop him in his quest.

Sara saw the frustration carving lines into his lean cheeks. His dark eyes reminded her of dark

119

embers of charcoal, burning, scorching her with their heat.

Then he did the most incredibly sexy thing. With razor-thin fingernails he opened the stitched seam one thread at a time, and pushed aside her panties. His patience had ended. One way or another he wanted to take her to the peak of passion.

The heel of his hand, his thrusting fingers, ministered to her lavishly. A deep, purring sound bubbled from between her lips into his mouth. He matched it with a low, husky growl. She matched his tempo; he caressed her harder, faster, deeper.

Her lips parting, Ryan watched the first signs of pleasure in the depths of her eyes with fascination. He realized he had never observed how intensely erotic it was to see the effect his love-making had.

"We'll make love with the lights on from now on. God, woman, you're beautiful." His palm ground against her. "And you're mine."

"A sneak preview of your intentions?" Sara asked, grinning gamely.

Ryan attempted to laugh at her quip, but his emotions still ran too high. "I'm going to love you until you beg me to stop."

"Sounds . . . divine. I guess I don't have to worry about what to wear for the occasion, do I?"

"That depends on how daring you are? I wouldn't be averse to something black and slinky, preferably *very* sheer with no clasps, buttons, or ties." He concentrated on closing her top button and restoring her to some semblance of order.

"Making up for lost time?"

"No, love. Insuring myself against future lost time. It's wasted on unbuckling, unbuttoning, and untying. Last night I actually found myself praying you wouldn't walk out on me." He shook his head at once again opening the wound that had festered for months.

"Trust me," Sara whispered. "I couldn't hurt you without hurting myself even more."

Ryan softly kissed her. "I have to trust you, Sara. I'm as close to being in love with you as humanly possible."

"Just close?"

"How about you?" Ryan answered with a question.

Sara stepped back two paces. She could lie and tell him she loved him without reservation, but in the back of her mind her conscience refused to allow the travesty. She wanted him, wanted to love him, and barring the ugly suspicions she had, she could. And yet the simple phrase lodged in her throat.

"I'm close," she said, temporizing.

Too close for comfort, she silently added. She needed a phone call from the main bank before she could commit herself any further than she had already.

CHAPTER SEVEN

"Sara, I need you."

She recognized Elizabeth's voice immediately. Elizabeth needed someone? Self-sufficient, sane Elizabeth Sheffield?

"Can I come over?"

"Of course. God knows you've always put up with me. How could I refuse?" Sara answered soberly.

"Five minutes?"

"I'll be here," Sara replied, at the same time reaching for the telephone directory.

Once the line had been disconnected, Sara tried to remember the bank's number, but as usual, she couldn't. How could a person who worked with numbers throughout the day be unable to remember the phone number of the place she worked in every day? Worse, she couldn't recite her own number. Silently cursing the mental block that kept her from remembering seven digits in a row, she opened the Yellow Pages to "Banks."

She glanced at her watch. *Don't let the re-corder be on yet,* she thought.

"Thank you for calling the People's—" Sara disconnected the line.

"Damn!"

In haste, wanting to contact Ryan and tell him she'd be late, she flicked through the five-inch-thick Houston white pages. "Crosby, Crosby, Crosby," she muttered. Finger skimming the multitude of Crosbys, she found she had a choice of R. E. Crosby, R. R. Crosby, and R. S. Crosby. *Why isn't life simple?* she thought despairingly when she saw they were all in the bay area.

"I'll recognize his voice," she said aloud, confident.

In rapid succession she jabbed in the numbers.

"Crosby residence," a feminine voice answered.

"Sorry, wrong number," Sara grumbled, hanging up.

She repeated the procedure with another number, and once again a woman answered the phone. Hanging up, Sara tried again, muttering, "Okay, R. S. Crosby. Be there!"

The sultriest sex-kitten voice Sara had ever heard came over the line. Expecting to hear Ryan's voice, Sara held the phone away from her ear and glared at it.

"Is this the No-Sense-of-Humor Crosby residence?" Sara purred.

"You must have the wrong number, darlin'. I keep the ship's captain smilin'."

Sara slammed the phone down with vehemence. Her eyes narrowing, her eight well-manicured nails digging into the palm of her hand, she felt only shafts of jealous pangs. "I keep the captain smilin'," she misquoted, simpering in a deep Texas accent. "Where were you when the bank needed christening? Jeez, I free the man of his personal demons, and he changes into a—"

Elizabeth opened the front door and poked her head in. "Sara? Who are you talking to?"

"An idiot! *Myself!*" Sara shouted.

"The idiot was on the other side of your front door," Elizabeth whispered. "I've done something terrible."

Sara directed her red-headed, well-stacked friend to the brightly colored sofa. "Jared McKnight? I thought everything was smooth as glass between the two of you."

"Remember the three-dimensional unicorn I designed? The one I planned to market exclusively to the top jewelry stores?" A tear slowly trickled down Elizabeth's cheek as she watched Sara nod her head. "He mass-produced the unicorn charm without consulting me." She groaned as she tucked one slender leg under herself before slumping to the sofa. "So I wrote a letter of resignation and left it on his desk. He wasn't supposed to find it until after the reception on Saturday. But he came back from Austin early and found it."

"Why do I have the feeling you've left out the spicy ingredients in the story?" Sara asked, delving deeper for the elusive facts Elizabeth concealed.

"I'm certain he reproduced the charm because . . ." She rubbed her forehead and hid her eyes from her close friend.

"Because?"

"I made a Sara Hawkins type of bet with him," she replied in a whispery voice. "I bet him he'd beg to crawl into my bed before I did. Oh, Sara. I'm the beggar."

"Elizabeth, you've called me a scatterbrained nitwit for years. I'm the last person you should emulate."

"When he read my one-line letter of resignation that said, 'Take this job and shove it,' he blew his cork. And . . ." She sniffled, ashamed to tell her the condition she'd left Jared McKnight in when she left the office. "I bopped him in the eye, too . . . accidentally."

"You? You hit someone? Don't blame that on me," Sara protested. "In my wildest escapades I've never resorted to violence." Her mind flashed to Ryan Crosby. She visualized a slender blond pussycat curled up in the cabin of his sailboat; her painted red toenails slithering between the calves of the captain's legs. "Maybe you did the right thing."

"You have the meanest look in your eyes."

Sara blinked away her own problem. "Anybody who upsets you deserves two black eyes—not one. You're a saint compared to me." Sara grinned. Elizabeth was down in the mouth. She needed to buoy her spirits. Teasing, she quipped, "I've always referred to you as my knockout friend. Guess there is more than a tinge of truth in the description."

Her lips drooping further instead of rising into a smile, Elizabeth visibly winced.

"You're an angel," Sara stated firmly.

"An angel with busted knuckles?" Elizabeth scoffed, holding out her right hand for inspection.

"You pack a mean wallop." A note of admiration in Sara's voice made Elizabeth's reddish eyebrows raise.

"His exact words before he sent me to the employee's cafeteria to get a bag of ice and a piece of raw beef. Then he extracted a promise I'm scared to death to keep."

Sara reached across the cushion between them and comfortingly laid her hand over her friend's. "You don't owe him anything. Promises under coercion don't count."

"I've told myself that, but I . . ." She cleared her throat, but Sara saw the glistening of tears in her eyes. "Oh, Sara! You would have invented some windy story, or laughed, or used some sense. I blew it! I punched him when he showed me a quality reproduction of my work."

Sara watched Elizabeth straighten her shoulders, thrust her chin forward decisively. "I'm going to that reception. I may be Jell-O on the inside, but I'm going to keep the last promise I made. You're going, too!"

"Now wait a minute, I wasn't invited."

126

"Yes, you were. Didn't you get the invitation in the mail?"

Her unopened mail lay on the dining-room table. Anxious to pack her purse and rush to Ryan's sailboat, she'd tossed it aside.

"It's probably in today's mail. Will my going help you face him?"

Elizabeth nodded her head. "You did get me into this to begin with," she added to convince Sara to accept. "Bring No-Sense-of-Humor Crosby."

"A dead carcass stinks." Sara snorted. "If mild-mannered Elizabeth Sheffield can give Jared McKnight a shiner, with my reputation for doing the outrageous, Ryan Crosby's life isn't worth a plugged nickel."

Laughing for the first time since entering Sara's condo, Elizabeth rose to her feet. "You'll think of something less mundane. The newspapers are filled with pistol-packin' Texans riddling holes in unsuspecting souls. Scissors are more your style anyway."

"They're great on ties but unsuitable for whittling a man back down to size."

"If I know you, you'll think of something clever." Elizabeth sighed. "I wish I had. Jared picked himself off the floor and grinned at me. He's going to get even rather than get mad." She crossed to the door, opened it, and paused. "Could you be there early Saturday?"

"I could think up a dandy little trick you could pull on him between now and then," Sara said, the twinkle back in her eyes.

127

"Save it for Crosby. Don't embezzle any bad checks," Elizabeth said jokingly, wiggling her fingers as a parting wave before closing the door.

The standing joke fell flat on Sara's ears. Embezzling wasn't something she kidded about now. Not when she conjectured about who had switched the funds in a customer's account. The computer system's being down at the main bank thwarted her from getting the answers she needed to find out who the culprit was.

Time and time again during the lull that afternoon she had made a mental list of who could have misappropriated the money. She blocked the name Ryan Crosby from appearing. She ticked off the remaining suspects and scratched off their names one by one. None of them other than the customer, herself, and the vice-president in charge of banking operations had access to the records necessary.

"Ryan Crosby!" she groaned, inwardly flinching with guilt at being too cowardly to confront him directly with the statement hidden in her teller's cage. "Two-timing, unprincipled . . . rascal!"

Although she said the words out loud, she couldn't bring herself to believe them. Why? she wondered. All the evidence pointed to either him or her, and she knew she hadn't done it, so . . .

"The green streak down your back is showing," she muttered. Some cutesy-butt answered his phone, and Sara had convicted Ryan of pilfering money!

Disgusted with herself and her wild imagination, she decided to give R. S. Crosby another call. The telephone directory still lay open on the table.

If Miss Sultry-Texas answered the phone, she thought angrily as she jabbed the number into the phone, Sara'd call a fellow she had once dated, a Houston cop, have Ryan arrested for indecent exposure!

The ringing tone buzzed in her ear. On the fifth ring a deep baritone voice answered, "Randy Crosby."

"Randy?" Sara squeaked, relieved.

"Yes, ma'am," the unknown man drawled. "What can I do for you, darlin'? Who is this?"

"You don't know me." Sara had begun to explain when the man interrupted.

"But I'd like to from the sound of your voice. Liquid velvet, babe, dark, smooth, and mysterious."

Sara giggled. "You're docked on Clear Lake, aren't you?"

"Yes, ma'am. Come on over. The rope latch is out."

"Well, uh, yes, I mean . . ." Flustered by his open invitation to a complete stranger, she didn't know what she meant. Under other circumstances curiosity would have forced her to spin a whirlwind of a tale and to suggest he come to the bank for inspection before she went

129

out with him. But her curiosity centered on Ryan, not on Randy.

"Do you know a Ryan Crosby per chance?"

"Sure. He's griped about taking my calls for months. One of us is going to have to change our phone listing. He's under 'J. Ryan Crosby' for future reference. I'd hate to have him miss a call from a gorgeous woman like you. Unless, of course, you're interested in meeting an attractive, available hunk."

"No, thanks. I'm so fantastically beautiful I don't want competition from the men I date."

"Hang on a second. I think I see Ryan pacing in front of his boat."

She could hear him bellowing Ryan's name. In a sexy, soft voice he whispered, "I'm docked three boats north of Ryan's if you change your mind."

"I won't."

Impatient to tell Ryan why she hadn't been dockside more than half an hour ago, she strummed her fingers.

"Sara?"

"How did you know who it was?"

"Who else would Randolph describe as the lady with the chocolate syrup voice?" He chuckled when he heard a quick intake of air. "Where are you?"

"Home."

"One of your saving graces is punctuality. Why aren't you here?"

Vastly relieved at being wrong about Ryan,

she partially excused his poke at her character. "It's your fault I couldn't call."

"Uh-huh. I also made you drop the tray of quarters. You're starting to attach my name to every disaster in your life. Does that mean"—his pause indicated the significance of the question and the fact that others were listening—"we're getting closer?"

"Your life was in peril when Sexy-Voice-Personified answered this number," she said teasingly. Suddenly Sara realized she was talking to him on the phone when she could be cuddled up next to him, having the same conversation. "I'll be there shortly unless you keep me on the phone and make me late."

"My fault again?" he asked, mock exasperation lacing his voice. Sara could almost see the lopsided grin on his face. "Hurry."

On the run Sara picked up the purse she had packed earlier with the world's skimpiest baby doll nightgown and gave herself a once-over in the mirror beside the door. No snaps. No buttons. No ties. The coral pink terry-cloth shorts outfit filled the bill. She patted what she jokingly called her rear patio with an ounce of dismay.

"Curves are better," she announced decisively. "Ya look beeee-you-tiful," she twanged in a poor imitation of James Cagney.

Any doubts she had had about her appearance were erased when she saw the expression on Ryan's face as she lightly ran down the dock and agilely jumped aboard his sailboat. He hugged her fiercely as she swung him around and around with pure joy in her heart.

"I'm getting dizzy," she squealed, but hung on tightly to his waist.

"My fault you're a dizzy blonde?" Ryan tossed his head back and laughed. "I hope your blaming me for everything you do is a genetic fault."

"Don't be fooled by the mop of blond curls. It's pretty shrewd to have a man accept responsibility for my actions, hmmmm?" She winked. Her hands slid from his sea blue shirt up to his face. "My dad loves being wrong. Perhaps it is hereditary for the women in the family always to be faultless."

Ryan groaned aloud at her logic. "My neighbor is anxious to meet you."

"I have other things planned," she whispered, nibbling love bites down the side of his throat.

"Turn around and wave," he said with a husky chuckle.

Sara shook her head. The imp inside her made her respond, "You'd be jealous if you knew what Mr. Hunk said to me."

"The way you were jealous of the woman who answered the phone?" Ryan used his whipcord strength trying to lift her off her feet but succeeded only in turning her so that she faced the boats on their right. "Are they waving?"

"You mean the bald man with the middle-aged paunch and the woman who looks like my grandmother?"

"That's the Mr. Hunk and Mrs. Sultry-Voiced-

Personified," Ryan managed to get out between laughs. "Still certain I'll be jealous?"

Raising one hand, Sara waved at the couple. "What's a rope latch?" she asked with faked innocence.

"Some boats don't have regular metal door latches because of the effect salt air has on the metal. Instead, there is a hole with a rope."

"Ahhhh." Her hot breath blew against his ear with a provocative caress. "I guess when the rope latch is out, it means—"

Ryan moved his head to block her view of the couple. "Why, that lecherous old coot!"

It was Sara's turn to throw her head back and laugh. "Is that jealousy or seasickness turning your complexion bright green?"

Her quip earned her a well-earned pinch on the rear patio. Sara nipped his earlobe in retaliation.

"Why did you torment me by being late?" he asked, rubbing the place he had pretended to injure.

"Remember my mentioning Elizabeth Sheffield?"

"Your neighbor."

"And childhood friend. She had a problem. I tried to call." Her choppy thoughts matched the strokes of his hand. His hold relaxed, and he lowered her feet to the deck.

"My number is 555-6242."

"I'll never remember it. I have a mental block against numbers seven digits long."

"Area code 713. Ten numbers."

Her face lit up. "Why didn't I think to break the seven barrier? That solves my phone problem."

"You truly are a lovable nut," Ryan commented, ruefully shaking his head.

"Bingo! You said the magic word." Sara flicked an imaginary cigar and wiggled her eyebrows. Without explaining, she opened her purse and held up a small jar of dry roasted peanuts. After twisting the jar open, she popped one in her mouth, then offered him some.

"Not this time. Last night I burned dinner—"

"That wasn't the only thing sizzling around here," Sara said, interrupting with a devilish grin.

"Tonight we're going to eat first." He pointed one tapered finger to the small table set by the railing. "Note, the knife and fork are properly placed. The wine is chilling in an ice bucket. Everything is perfect for an intimate tête-à-tête."

With a courtly swirl of the linen napkin on her plate, he held back her chair and waited for her to be seated. "I've planned a full four-course meal."

"Hmmmmm." Sara slid into the chair.

"Salad with a special blue cheese dressing." He picked up a walnut bowl and began tossing the ingredients.

"My favorite."

"Followed by fresh seafood gumbo." Twirling the forks dramatically, he served her a heaping pile of fresh greens, then held the pepper

134

grinder in front of her. She nodded. "And completed with broiled flounder, lightly basted with butter, stuffed with flaky crabmeat."

"What's the fourth course?" she asked, hoping she knew what he planned on serving for dessert: Ryan Crosby à la nude.

"Homemade apple cobbler."

Her lips pouting in disappointment, Sara picked up her fork. "Dinner is going to take hours," she said complainingly. "Soup and sandwich would have been fine."

Ryan served himself and sat down. His knees settled against her thigh. "I thought you'd be delighted."

"Oh, I am," Sara replied grumpily. "Next, you'll want to gossip about what's going on at work."

"Did you know Sharon is pregnant?"

"Can't be. The salad dressing is delicious."

Laughing, Ryan dabbed at his mouth before sipping his wine. "You mix your topics constantly, don't you?"

Sara glanced up and admired the laugh creases beside his eyes. "I guess. But you knew what I meant."

"Why can't Sharon be pregnant? Blue cheese is my favorite," he said, keeping both topics strung together the way she had.

"I hate mayonnaise-based salad dressing. She isn't married."

"You switched the order of your answers."

"So?" Sara switched the food from one side of

135

her mouth to the other while spearing another piece of lettuce on her fork.

"I'm just trying to follow your line of thinking," Ryan explained.

If he felt free to pick her mind apart, she decided to do a little picking herself. "Since you're in on all the latest gossip, have you heard the rumor about the embezzler?"

She waited to hear his fork drop on the plate. It didn't. He didn't even have the grace to take in a deep breath of air. Much to her dismay, he kept on chewing as though she had mentioned how lovely the weather was.

"I've heard you joking around with the customers about taking a cut of their deposits. Is this a confession?"

Ryan swallowed the ball of smashed lettuce with difficulty. With the greatest amount of self-control he could muster up, he smiled in her direction. He'd offered to help her out of any financial jam she'd gotten herself into. Was she finally going to take him up on it?

"Remember how we pretended to be the hero and heroine in a bodice ripper last night?" She peeked out from beneath her long lashes and saw him nod. "Let's talk about committing the perfect crime. Say my aging mother is terminally ill, without hospital coverage, and I desperately need some ready cash. How would I go about getting it?"

"Is your mother ill?" he asked in an effort to separate truth from fiction.

"No. We're pretending."

"Hmmmm." He poked another forkful of salad in his mouth and chewed thoughtfully. "Tellers have ready access to the cash."

"Too obvious. Be devious."

"I'd keep track of customers who didn't keep accurate records and some way or another snatch a bit here and a bit there. Never enough to overdraw the account but, combined, enough to meet the hospital expenses."

"Major flaw. When you switched their money by means of altering figures, you'd have a zillion entries on your own account."

"Okay, mastermind, how would you do it?"

"Your idea about keeping track of customers is a good one. Only I'd monitor the ones who didn't use their accounts. Say, a person or company savings account."

Ryan gave up on the pretense of eating. She was going to tell him how to embezzle, and he didn't intend to miss a single word. "Let me think. What is the easiest way to get access to an account?"

"The Impact card?" Sara hadn't thought of that possibility. The customers who did manage to get their accounts screwed up generally found the rectangular pieces of silver plastic the culprit. They'd make withdrawals and forget to enter the amounts into their records.

"Two fallacies. One, you have to have the card. Two, you have to know the pin number."

Sara laughed. "Have you any idea how many customers use their Impact cards as identification to cash checks and forget to get them back?

137

I have a ledger book full of names of people who have had their cards mailed to the bank. And what about the Impact machines throughout the United States that manage to gobble up cards?"

"It doesn't happen that often."

"Computers are programmed to accept only perfect cards. Scratch it, chip off a corner, deface it, and the computer snarfs it down. Happens constantly," Sara said.

"But you still have the problem of learning the pin number, don't you? We don't have any record of the numbers at the bank."

"Simple. Ask the customer."

"Would he tell you?"

"Sure. I'm considered an official of the bank. Why would anyone doubt me?"

Ryan stared at her intensely. The pieces of the puzzle clipped into place, but she hadn't explained the last detail. "Isn't there a record book you keep showing when the card came in, when you called the customer, and when he picked the card up?"

"I'm ready for gumbo." Sara didn't want to talk about a hypothetical case. She wanted to know how he could do it.

"Yeah, sure," Ryan replied, rising and going into the cabin.

First thing tomorrow morning he planned to get hold of the ledger book she'd spoken of. A feeling of dread rather than anticipation seeped into his pores. He had to know for certain. There wasn't room for reasonable doubt.

His lips pressed together in a straight line, he had a gut feeling that in some way the ledger had been altered. Sara, unashamed, had confessed to the crime. Although he heard the words from her own mouth, he couldn't believe her capable of committing a crime. Dammit, she just wasn't the type!

He ladled a cup of the chunky soup into a bowl. Why? There had to be a motive, some reasonable explanation for stealing from the bank.

"Sara, have you ever thought about what you'd do with a big wad of extra money?" he asked removing her salad plate and replacing it with the steaming gumbo.

"No." Hawaiian steel guitars droned in her imagination. She recalled an African setting with Ryan Crosby playing the lead role as the daring hunter. "Well, yes, I have come to think of it. But first of all, I'd have to figure out a way to get the money into an account that wasn't traceable."

Give a little to get a little, she thought, justifying her admission of dreaming about spending someone else's money. She needed to know how he had managed to keep his bank statement clean of corresponding entries.

"Remember the trouble you had finding my correct phone number? I could easily open an account as J. R. Crosby. Or a married woman could open one under her maiden name."

Sara narrowed her eyes as she contemplated getting down to the printout machine first thing in the morning to check out J. R. Crosby's account. He hadn't used the Impact card method to swipe money from the bank, but once she had her hands on the printout, she'd be able to figure out how he did it.

"What would you do with the money?" She probed with what she hoped was an innocent expression on her face.

"I never thought about it," he replied smoothly.

"Huh! Anybody who works in a bank has had it cross his mind. When you were in the vault, you were fingering the cash like an unsupervised kid in a candy factory."

"Now, Sara, that's your interpretation. You also listened to Mr. Hunk and pictured him as six feet tall, biceps out to here." He etched a muscle of mountainous size over his own bicep. "What you heard didn't coincide with Ma and Pa Kettle three boats down, did it?"

A teasing light entered her eyes. "Nope. But it's all your fault."

"My fault! You fantasize about spending someone else's money, and it's my fault? What kind of logic is that?"

"How do you think I paid for the expensive tie I had to replace? I have more time than I have money. The last week of the month I'm always broke. I had to get the money from somewhere."

"Now you're kidding me, aren't you?"

Sara picked up her soup spoon and rapped his knuckles. "I've been pretending or kidding since *you* brought up the topic of bank gossip." Her eyes drilled into his. "Haven't you?"

"Of course," Ryan lied. "But don't blame the topic of conversation on me. I mentioned Sharon's pregnancy. You brought up embezzling."

As an inventor of whopping stories Sara recognized a bold-faced lie when she heard it. He hadn't been kidding. What had he been probing for? A new wrinkle? An infallible means of dipping further into customers' accounts without detection?

No way, Mr. Triple-Dipping Crosby. You think I have the ledger and can be cajoled into helping you, but you're wrong on both counts, Sara thought as she chased a shrimp around the edge of the bowl. Appetite gone, she mentally flogged herself for falling in love with a criminal.

"Sara?" Ryan intruded softly into her silence. They both had tiptoed around the issue too long. He couldn't wait until tomorrow morning to get her out of her cage slyly, then to sneak in and check the ledger. He had to know . . . now. "Did you ever take anything that didn't belong to you?"

CHAPTER EIGHT

An oyster jumping out of its shell from the depths of the bay and landing beside the cooked shrimp she chased with her spoon couldn't have surprised Sara more. She fully understood how Always-in-Control Elizabeth Sheffield had lost her cool and given Jared McKnight a black eye. Ryan Crosby had the nerve to ask her if *she* had ever taken anything that didn't belong to her. No doubt he wanted references before he included her in on his take from the bank.

How had Elizabeth said she would react in a stress situation? With a joke, a smile, or some sense? She'd give him a little of each, and then she'd get the hell out of here, Sara decided.

Assuming an appropriate nervousness in her tone, she answered, "Once."

Ryan closed his eyes with relief. Once he knew what, why, and how, he could help her. He would personally go to the president of the bank and plead her case. Surely, as well liked as Sara was, his boss would not press charges.

"Tell me about it," Ryan prompted.

He wanted an accomplished thief? She'd give him one hell of an accomplishment!

"I couldn't help myself," she said with a pitiful whine, dropping her spoon in the gumbo and watching the soup splash over the side on his white linen tablecloth.

"I saw the money there. I looked all the way around the room and nobody was watching. I could almost hear it say, 'Take me, take me.' What good was it doing anybody just lying there?"

Ryan sighed. Now he knew why she had taken the money from inactive accounts. She felt the customers weren't using the cash, so she might as well. *Oh, Sara.* He silently groaned.

"I touched it." She scooted her chair back, slumped her shoulders dejectedly. "The voice said louder, 'Think what I can buy if I'm yours!' Back then I lived in a tiny efficiency apartment, poorly furnished, near starvation on my salary. Do you think you could get me a raise?" she asked, using her usually double line of reasoning to throw Ryan off the track while she plotted a fitting ending for her ridiculous lie. From the corner of her eye she saw the shocked expression on his face.

"Let's worry about your keeping your job, okay?" Ryan suggested, placing his hand lightly on her arm.

Sure, Clyde, she answered him silently. *You wouldn't want Bonnie to lose her inside track, would you? Or draw attention to herself by dunning the boss for a raise?* Sara concentrated

143

on keeping her hand relaxed, not using it to swipe away his loathsome touch.

She sniffled and moved her arm away from beneath his fingers to pick up a napkin and blow her nose. A honking shrimp boat lost in a fog would have been quieter.

"You're a rat fink to make me tell you this," she whispered dramatically.

She wiped her lipstick on the napkin. Her eyes searched for something to destroy before departing. They landed on the matching crystal salt and pepper shakers. When she dropped the napkin, she idly picked up the salt shaker and twirled it around and around at the edge of the table as though she were nervous.

"I'm going to help you." He reassured her in a soothing voice. "Tell me how you did it."

"I picked it up an stuffed it in my purse," she answered as though he had asked the dumbest question in the world.

Going to help her? She scoffed to herself. She was going to help him a bit. The salt shaker dropped to the deck and shattered to smithereens. "Oh, Ryan, look what I've done! I'm so sorry."

She brought her right arm across the table, swiping off the crystal wineglasses as it passed over the dishes. Ryan jumped to his feet but wasn't fast enough to keep the white wine from splashing on his light-colored pants. As she reached over to dab at the stain, her fingers purposely caught the edge of the tablecloth and pulled it to his front.

More help on the way, she thought, crowing to herself.

"Oh!" she gasped, standing, bringing the corner of the cloth to cover her mouth. "I'm such a klutz when I talk about this!" she wailed over the sound of china, crystal, and silverware crashing to the floor.

"It's all right, Sara. Don't move. I'll get the broom and dustpan. Do you want to go in and lie down?"

The offer was appealing. A wrecking ball couldn't have done a more thorough job on the back deck. With each mincing step she took, his fine dinnerware crunched beneath her feet. Ten minutes alone in the cabin, and she could probably sink the whole damned ship.

"No." She didn't want to get trapped below in the bow of the ship with the single escape route blocked by Ryan. "Can't I do anything to help?"

Ryan surveyed the damage. Not a single dish could be salvaged. Her fidgeting feet were grinding the food and crystal into the finish of the deck. "No. Let me help you onto the dock while I clean up the mess."

Slipping and sliding her feet as much as possible, she made certain the soup on the bottom of her shoes left a gooey trail.

"My purse, please."

"Don't worry about your purse. It's safe."

"Nuts!" Sara yelled. "You know how hungry I get when I'm upset. The nuts are in my purse."

Sara wiped her shoes on the side of the boat when she climbed out. As she turned around to

145

view the disaster from above, a gleam of triumph shone in her eyes. Watching Ryan tiptoe through the disaster area to retrieve her purse brought her lips up into a smile of glee. She schooled her face in a pitiful expression before he turned around, purse in hand.

"We'll finish our discussion after I've scraped up dinner," Ryan muttered to himself, but Sara overheard him.

Fat chance, buster, Sara thought, wishing he'd lose his footing. A doctor at the hospital would have to use tweezers to remove the teeny shards of glass from his rump.

"Now you stand there while I get something to clean this up with. Okay?" Ryan asked solicitously.

Sara delved into her purse, searching for a pen and notepad. The moment he disappeared into the cabin, she scribbled a short note, flung it into the middle of the mess, where it couldn't be missed, and fled from the dock.

Once she had managed to get back to her condo, the anger she had concealed with her whopping lie surfaced. She slammed the door hard enough to make the pictures on the wall jar.

"Sara, I care for you. I'm close to falling in love with you." She mimicked Ryan in disdain. "I'm going to take you to prison with me on our honeymoon. We won't waste time with buttons, clasps, or ties. A prison uniform you just slip over your head!"

The phone began ringing. Sara stopped her

146

tirade to debate whether or not to answer it. She was safe in her own home. There wasn't anything Crosby-the-Thief could do to her. Why not answer it?

"Helloooo," she crooned into the receiver, imitating the voice of the sexy grandmother down the dock from Ryan.

"What the hell do you mean by the crown jewels are safe in the Tower of London?" Ryan roared.

"That's what I was tempted to steal. How's that for references, you . . ." she sputtered, biting back foul expletives.

"References?" he yelled louder.

"Isn't that what the grand inquisition was all about? Get her to confess an adolescent crime like shoplifting, then blackmail the dummy into helping *you* with *your* embezzling? What kind of fool do you think I am?"

"You think I'm the embezzler?" he squawked, his voice breaking with incredulous shock. "Me?"

"Well, it sure as hell isn't me," Sara said huffily. "That computer razzmatazz you confessed to told me exactly how you do it?"

Sara heard a burst of harsh laughter. "Don't try to set me up as the scapegoat for *your* crimes."

"What? Are you telling me you think *I'm* the one with sticky fingers? Of all the damned nerve!"

She slammed the phone down, hoping it would break his eardrum. Seconds later it began ringing again. Sara pulled the plug from the wall. The silence was deafening. Sara strode over and turned on the television set.

Ignoring the latest episode of *Dallas,* she recapped the eventful evening. Ryan thought she had embezzled the money all by herself! He didn't want to be a modern-day version of a highwayman with his female companion. That was too romantic. She wouldn't even get credit for robbing the rich to save the poor. He thought she was cramming money between her boobs to buy—her arms swept around the room while she searched for the right word—fripperies! That explained everything. It explained why he had changed from No-Sense-of-Humor Crosby to Lover-Boy-of-the-Century!

And what did you do when you suspected him? a devilish inner voice asked.

"That's different. I've loved the skunk for months!"

Loved? What kind of love allows room for suspicion of criminal activity?

"Dammit, I don't know that he's innocent. He could have pretended to be innocent just the way he pretended to care about me."

Sara and her conscience paced back and forth, side by side.

Did he pretend?

"Of course he did. I knew all along he was trying to use me. I merely had the wrong reason attached. Here I thought he was looking for a partner in crime, and he was looking for the criminal! How wrong can you be?"

How wrong are you now? You have been known to go off half-cocked, jumping to the wrong conclusion.

"Minor errors in judgment. What was I supposed to think when I saw him playing with the money down in the vault?"

He could have been straightening up the mess you made when you shoved it in there.

Sara winced. Along with his multitude of lectures about her cash drawer, he had reprimanded her about keeping the cash in the vault neatly stacked by denominations. She chalked a score of one up for her conscience.

"But he made love to me," she argued, voice shaking into a low whisper. "What kind of man makes love to a woman when he thinks she's a thief?"

What kind of woman makes love to a man when she thinks he's a thief?

Her pacing took her to the mirror in front of the door. "Whose side are you on?" she demanded of her alter ego. "I wasn't thinking about money once he kissed me. I wasn't thinking . . . period."

Excuses, excuses. What are you going to do? Cry? Mope around? Find some way to make everything his fault the way you usually do?

"There's nothing else I can do," she whispered despondently.

Like hell. Where's your spunk? Are you going to let him get away with thinking you're the guilty party?

"No!"

Well?

Sara turned her back on the mirror. The grandfather clock chimed eleven times. There was one way to prove herself innocent. Find the guilty party. But how? She began pacing around the oval cocktail table. She had one tangible clue: the quarterly savings statement. But that was at the bank in her cage.

A hunger pang sliced across her waist. Automatically she went to her purse to retrieve the jar of nuts. Deep in thought, she opened the jar and popped a handful into her mouth.

She remembered telling Ryan she could think clearly when her mouth was full. One of the few truths she had told, she realized glumly. She had told him enough windy tales to compete with a force ten hurricane. No wonder he thought she was capable of stealing. Liars and thieves go hand in hand.

Mentally she clamped a lid on her conscience and indulged in self-pity. One of the few things she felt she had going for her was her sense of the ridiculous. She compensated for not being the slimmest girl in town by being the funniest girl in town.

"A clown," she muttered after she had swallowed, "hiding behind a mask made of smiles."

Sara collapsed on the sofa. Her knee bent, one leg propped up on the other, she balanced the jar on her belly. She should have known he was up to something when he insinuated she was fat, then invited himself over to her apartment. What did he think he was? An American version of the Russian KGB? Did he think he could solve the crime by sleeping with her?

Why? What had she ever said or done to make him think she'd steal from the bank? Just because she'd told half the clientele she was taking ten to fifteen percent of their deposits? Just because she had the nerve to clip his tie in half? Just because she'd dumped a hundred dollars' worth of quarters in the lobby on one of the busiest days of the month? Did that give anyone the right to suspect her?

Yes! that little voice affirmed.

"Oh, shut up. You're supposed to be on my side!"

The smile, a silver lining around her cloud of gloom, burst through. Mr. Crosby thought she was a thief, didn't he? While fervently proclaiming his innocence, he was deliberately, sneakily trying to trap her!

Wasn't he the genius who'd said, "Looks can be deceiving"? Well, Mr. Mensa Crosby, two can play your game. By God, she'd lead the police right up the garden path beside the boat dock and deliver the real thief when he answered her knock.

Was he the thief?

Sara shook her head. The same gut level feeling she'd had all along surfaced. He wasn't the thief, but he thought she was. Let him continue to malign her character. Informing him of who the embezzler was and how the embezzlement had been accomplished would bring him to his knees.

151

Mind whirling faster than the coin counter, Sara plotted her strategy. On that positive note, she ate the remainder of the peanuts while getting ready for bed. Throughout the night the phrase "Catch a thief" ran through her dreams. A smug smile curved her lips as she dreamed of the president of the bank's presenting her with a gold watch for cleverly apprehending the villain.

The next day her first order of business, before the bank doors opened, was to contact the main bank's headquarters. In some way she felt certain the answer to the puzzle lay in that single quarterly savings statement.

"There aren't any signed withdrawal slips," the woman she had spoken to the first time she had called days before droned in a bored voice. "Do you have the statement in front of you?"

"How do you get money out of the bank without a withdrawal slip? Of course, I have the statement in front of me," Sara replied curtly.

"See the column of seven digit numbers to the left? The code is on the back of the statement."

Sara jotted down the seven numbers that her brain refused to assimilate and flipped the sheet over. "Oh, my God! Of course there aren't any signed withdrawal slips. The Impact card was used."

"Right. If the card is used at another bank, the name of the bank is listed, but the card was used at the place it was issued, your branch, so only the number is given."

She rubbed her fingers across the frown line

in the center of her brow. "Thanks," Sara replied, adding silently, *I think.* "Bye."

Another line of consternation slit her forehead as she hung up the phone. Crissy? Maybe Crissy had used the card to "borrow" some company funds, then replaced them before the statement was due. What other explanation could there be?

Sara mentally denied the possibility as her thoughts returned to Ryan. He wouldn't have been stupid and picked up on only one account. There must be others she didn't know about. How was she going to find the other customer accounts which had illegal transactions posted? He had access to the daily computer sheets, but she did not.

Think, she ordered herself, trying to get past the stone wall impeding her progress. To call up each account, one by one, on her teller's machine would take forever. Her teeth clamped together, she realized the information on the computer sheets, checking the Impact transactions, would be the fastest, surest way to compile a list to check.

But how would she manage to get Ryan out of his office long enough to check the printouts? Wait a second, if he suspected someone of embezzling money, he most likely had a list of the tampered-with accounts.

Her eyes drifted over the front lobby toward Ryan, who strolled to the front doors to unlock them. His dark eyes made a final check to make certain the employees were at their stations, ready to wait on the customers. Had they lingered for a moment longer on her? Sara questioned, hoping they had.

He looked haggard. *Must have had a sleepless night,* she thought. A hint of a smile drew her lips up fractionally. The mess she had made should have taken him hours to clean up. Served him right, she mused, glancing down at her robin's egg blue suit with pristine ivory-colored blouse. Let him ponder why she looked hale and chipper. Damned KGB spy.

Recalling the discussion they had had the previous evening, she began tallying the questions he had asked her in view of the information she now had. Now that she knew Impact cards had been used, had she unknowingly given him the key pieces to the embezzling puzzle?

How would you get the card? he had asked. *Use the ones lost and returned to the bank. But how would you find out the pin number? Simple. Ask the customer.*

Sara took the line of questioning a step further. What about the ledger? When a card came back to the bank, the date it arrived and the date the customer was notified were meticulously entered. When the customer picked up the card, he or she signed the ledger.

The ledger! Months ago she had delegated the responsibility of keeping track of the lost card ledger to—Richard Grant? Head swiveling, eyes widening, she stared at the man who had received the Teller of the Year award the previous year.

154

Not Richard, she thought, refusing to put his name within the realm of possibility. Fussy, persnickety Richard Grant? He was the only man she'd ever met who wouldn't allow his body to sweat! She slightly shook her head. Richard Grant? The embezzler?

While she disclaimed the probability, another thought entered her mind. She wouldn't have to figure out some sly way to get the list of customers from the computer sheets. If the embezzler, some way or another, was using the lost Impact cards, she had easy access to the ledger. She merely had to ask for it.

Merely? Sara snorted at the naïveté. She hadn't checked the ledger for ages. All of a sudden, out of the clear blue, she'd ask for it? He'd know. Worse, he'd know she knew. Then how would she check it out without his becoming suspicious? *Wait until he's out of his cage to sneak a peek* was the logical reply.

A rush of excitement tingled through her from her head to her toes to her fingertips. She had to get her hands on the ledger. But doing so, without detection, wouldn't be easy during working hours.

What about after work? Grant managed to balance to the penny by quitting time. She could wait until he left, then snatch the ledger. Pleased with the idea of having the answer-providing pages within six hours' grasp, Sara turned back to the front of the cage. *Patience, my dear, patience,* she told herself.

Whereas yesterday the lobby was swamped

with customers, today they straggled in. She glanced at the glass partition in Ryan's office and wondered what he had done with the information she had given him. If they hadn't been personally involved, she could have almost forgiven him for suspecting her. Lost Impact cards fell within the realm of her responsibility.

For several seconds their eyes met and held. He leaned forward, propping his elbows on the desktop, his hands beneath his chin. One finger crooked and beckoned her to come to his office.

She hooked her heels on the rung of the stool and rose so he could see all of her face.

Business or pleasure? she mouthed in exaggeration in hope he could read her lips.

His finger pointed to himself. *Me boss.* He raised his hand and pointed in her direction. *You employee.*

Her lips thinning into a straight line, she scowled and curtly nodded her head. During the night she had decided exactly how she would react to any overtures on his part. She'd give him a taste of the dumb blonde routine: Show abject humbleness while she skewered him like a Texas-size shishkebob.

"May I sit down, sir?" she asked with a forced smile when she entered his office.

Ryan studied her body language when she perched on the chair on the opposite side of his desk. Her legs crossed at the ankles, her arms crossed over her chest, her body screeched, "I'm not telling you a damned thing."

"The weather is nice today, isn't it?" he asked benignly.

"A storm is brewing in the Gulf. Hurricane season is upon us," she answered, batting her eyes flirtatiously. "I'm terribly afraid of violent storms."

He read between the lines easily. This was the calm before the storm, but he wasn't the least bit afraid.

"Is the hatch buttoned down on your sailboat?" she asked solicitously.

What she meant was had he gotten the mess cleaned up, he thought, grinding his back molars. "Shipshape," he said.

"Good. I made a *terrible* mess, didn't I?"

"No worse than the mess I made of things." Ryan decided to cut through the social niceties. "Do you think I'm the embezzler?"

"Too bad you didn't eat more of the peanuts I brought. You'd have discovered my secret. I had several crumpled hundred-dollar bills in the bottom of the peanut jar," she said derisively. Sara leveled her eyes with his and gave him a chance at the same vile question he had thrown at her: "Do you think I'm capable of embezzling?"

He sidestepped the peanut story she had thrown out as a red herring. "Everything points in your direction, doesn't it?" he replied, weighing the facts truthfully.

"I believe you taught me an invaluable lesson: Appearances are deceptive."

Hadn't he appeared to be the attentive lover?

157

Hadn't he masqueraded as a man who had been deeply hurt? Hadn't he used his false insecurities to make her tell about outgrowing her own insecurities? Sara could justify anything she said or did by recalling the deceptive appearances he had given.

"Case in point being the rash of 'accidents' last night?" He rubbed his index knuckle against a strip of stubble beneath his chin he missed while shaving while trying to solve the mystery of Sara Hawkins at the same time. He should have stuck to shaving, he thought self-admonishingly. Finding out what made Sara tick would take a master watchmaker.

Again Sara flirtatiously batted her eyelashes in his direction. "I'm pure disaster when I'm upset."

Sara noticed the bags under his eyes she hadn't observed from a distance. He was baggy-eyed, grim-lipped, and poorly shaven, and she fought the urge to lean over and whisper to him about the agile bit of detective work she had accomplished. Ryan raked his fingers through his hair, and the gesture was almost her undoing. She had touched the dark wave near the crown of his head. She knew how soft, alluring it felt beneath her fingertips.

"Sara, you didn't do it, did you?" he asked quietly. "Somehow I can't believe you're guilty."

"Of taking the queen of England's crown jewels? Of course not."

"Okay, I'll play your game. Do you believe I took the crown jewels?"

She slowly rose to her feet. Purposely adding a strong flavor of pomposity to her voice, she replied, "Mr. Crosby, you're guilty of taking and abusing something of greater value than jewels or money. My reputation has greater worth to me than either of them."

Congratulating herself on the superb exit line, she stalked to the doorway self-righteously. Chin high, she thrust the final gibe at him. "Was there ever really a Susan? If mental cruelty was punishable by law, you'd be locked up longer than she would."

Without a backward glance she marched out of his office, leaving Ryan with the feeling she had given him a quick kick in his gut. He had questioned her basic integrity; she had reciprocated by implying he had based their relationship on a lie.

Ryan whistled a breath of air from his lungs. No one could accuse Sara Hawkins of not having gumption. The lady had every right to doubt his motivation. But what she didn't realize, Ryan mused, was that he'd been haunted by his suspicions rather than gloated over them. The bottom line, his love, had shielded her from his informing his superiors of the facts days ago. He had mentally pointed the accusing finger at every employee rather than accuse Sara.

"You screwed up," he mumbled.

Throughout the sleepless night he had cursed Sara for believing him capable of ripping the bank off, then cursed himself for practically accusing her of the same crime. By dawn the single conclusion he'd come to had shed a minuscule amount of light on the picture. They both had talked in circles from the beginning, but her motivation was pure, while his had dirty smudges around the edges. She'd never believe him any more than he gave credence to the bizarre stories she told.

Ryan thumped his desk with his knuckles and ridiculed his fact-finding mission. She had spun one of her wild tales, and he had latched onto it like a bank examiner presenting incriminating evidence to the bank's board of directors.

Today's confrontation hadn't helped matters. He felt certain he could get down on his belly and slither through the lobby and she would shout, "Poisonous snake. Kill the bastard," rather than listen to the logic behind his reasoning.

With luck, he would track down the culprit taking the money, but he doubted Sara would ever forgive him. Her final remark had the ring of finis.

CHAPTER NINE

Of all the days in the year, why does Richard Grant have to be out of balance by fifty-four cents today? Sara griped to herself as she locked her movable cart and prepared to roll it to the vault. She piddled around with a nearly empty box of matches on the counter, moving it first one way, then the other.

Some reward she was getting for being patient. She should have snatched the ledger while he was at lunch and taken her chances of getting caught. But oh, no, impetuous Sara Hawkins had decided she needed to practice restraint. And what had it got her? The big zero. She was standing there like a sore thumb, looking as suspicious as hell, while Grant figured out ways to cop millions from the bank. So much for patience.

"Can I help?" Sara offered.

"No, Sara. You run along home. I'm certain it's a transposition. I'll find it."

"But I switch numbers around all the time. I can find it faster than you can," she insisted.

"Why don't you roll my cart into the vault and I'll do a quick scan of the tapes?" *And other things,* she added to herself.

"My error. This will teach me not to rush, to be careful." Richard's glasses slipped to the end of his nose as he peered myopically over the partition separating their cages. "Don't worry, Sara. This won't take long."

A quick flash of guilt made her face feel warm. Could Grant be the thief? She questioned herself for the hundredth time. Why couldn't it be someone she disliked? Someone with sneaky eyes, bad breath, and a mean mouth would fit her idea of a crook. Poor Richard didn't resemble a criminal.

Sara tugged her cart out from under the counter, plunked her satchel purse on top, and began wheeling it to the vault. Once she'd clocked out, there wouldn't be any way to get back into the bank. She didn't have a key. Immediately she ruled out asking the night watchman to let her in. If she were wrong and someone were to find out she had returned to the bank after closing hours, she'd have some tall explaining to do. Whom could she trust to let her in without letting it slip if she was wrong?

Deep in thought, she practically ran Ryan down with her cart before she noticed him standing beside the open vault doors.

She started to apologize politely until he raised his hands, chuckled, and said, "I know. It's my fault for being in the way."

Her feet seemed glued to the floor with the

cart between them. Had the fates tossed Ryan Crosby in front of her in answer to her question? Realizing her mouth hung open, she snapped it shut.

"You wouldn't let me make up for the disaster last night by fixing dinner for you at my house, would you?" Sara made every effort to disguise her real reason for inviting him to dinner by giving him what she hoped was a repentant smile.

Ryan turned the money cart into the vault and pushed it into the neat row of identical carts, each distinguished by a number on the right-hand corner. When the cart left her hands, Sara found herself concentrating on what to do with them. Her eyes betrayed her by sliding to the door on the inner vault. The last thing she needed to distract her was thoughts of their previous interlude in the vault.

She laced her fingers together behind her back to keep them from also betraying her. The urge to touch him and to say, "Care to step into the cash vault and . . . count money?" hung behind her teeth, poised to plop out of her mouth.

Ryan pivoted around and caught the wistful expression on her cherubic face. Hours ago he had decided to come clean and ask for her help in solving the mystery, but he'd been afraid of being rebuffed. His suspicions made him morally bankrupt in her accounting book.

A few feet apart they both threw caution aside and closed the gap.

Arms wrapped around Sara, Ryan hunched down and murmured next to her ear, "I feel like Adlai Stevenson's shoe. There's a big hole in my soul."

"Me, too. I planned those verbal thrusts this morning, but I walked out bleeding myself," she mumbled against the silk tie pressed to her lips.

"I didn't believe you did it," they both chorused in unison.

"I was wrong," Sara whispered. "And this time it wasn't your fault."

"Oh, but it was. I should never have suspected you to begin with," Ryan said. "Don't fight those hereditary genes when I'm willing to accept the responsibility for being wrong."

"I'm still going to apologize," Sara happily argued.

"Apology duly noted but not accepted until you accept my apology first."

As they laughed and hugged each other, Sara blurted out, "But I know who did it! And I'll have to get back into the bank tonight to prove it."

"Okay. I'll help you. But first how about my taking you up on your dinner invitation, and then you can tell me what you've found out today. Frankly, I'm still stumped."

Sara wiggled out of his arms. "Sounds great. Much better than my figuring out a way to get back inside the bank tonight alone."

"I have to wait to lock up until everyone has left. Meet me outside in the parking lot?"

Ryan couldn't resist the warm smile on her

lips. Swiftly he captured them beneath his own, fearing their reconciliation was too good to be true. Along with his self-recrimination, he had discovered one golden thread throughout his thoughts: He loved Sara Hawkins. He could go through life being totally wrong, but he wanted Sara to be there to tell him it was all his fault.

"Richard Grant is searching for a transposition. By the time you're free to leave I can have dinner simmering on the stove. Why don't we meet at my place?"

"You're right . . . as usual," he said with an ear-to-ear grin. His hand lingered below her waist as she turned to head out of the vault. "You won't correct me if I tell you you have the cutest tush in town, will you?"

"Of course not. I've known that for years," she quipped, knowing full well he had told the biggest lie to date. She had to give him credit for one thing: He'd sounded as though his whopper held an underlying current of truth.

"Your purse," Ryan whispered. "We can't have you starving on the freeway on your way home."

Sara stretched on tiptoe and brushed her lips against his. "Hot dog!"

"In your purse?"

"No. For dinner. Something quick to fix. We have important business to take care of tonight."

She picked her purse straps out of his hands and swung it on her right forearm. The charming half-smile and arched blond eyebrow encouraged him to put any interpretation on the remark he chose. With either option, bed or bank, she hoped he wouldn't be wrong.

Practically running from the car into the condo, she screeched to a halt when she saw Elizabeth coming out of her door.

"Hi, Elizabeth! Is it still okay to invite Ryan to the reception?" Sara purposely lowered her eyelids to attain an air of mystery.

"No-Sense-of-Humor Crosby back in your good graces?" Elizabeth asked. "And here I thought you were planning foul play."

Might as well start practicing now, Sara thought. "You were right. Shootings are trite."

Elizabeth dramatically clutched her heart and leaned back against the papered wall. "I'm right? Can't be. I've been wrong since you swindled me out of that piece of apple pie in first grade. Didn't you tell me it was wrong to eat homemade dessert when all you had was a bagful of store-bought cookies?"

Sara giggled girlishly. "You wouldn't think I loved you if you were right all the time."

"Life is pretty rocky for me. I'm not certain I can adjust to being right for a change," Elizabeth said teasingly, looping her arm over her shorter friend's shoulder. "Don't ruin a perfect record by seeing more than one side of a picture. Next, we'll be able to carry on a five-minute conversation without my having to keep track of two topics at once."

"Wrong," Sara replied as expected. "You didn't give me a chance to ask about Jared."

Elizabeth squeezed Sara's arm. "I'm determined to keep the unicorn away from Jared's dime-store distribution. Saturday night's reception is the big kiss-off. I have rights, too."

"Was that a pun?" Sara said with a groan.

"Sure was," Elizabeth replied, a note of pride in her voice.

"Stick to being gorgeous and leave the humor to me," Sara advised, smiling. "It takes a double-track mind to handle a whopper."

"You're right; I'm wrong. Years of practice went into developing the knack of twisting an idiom or a slogan the way you do. Crosby can come to the reception."

"Thanks. Watch out using a double train of thought, too. Misunderstandings can be worse than state bank examiners," Sara warned, thinking of the problems she had encountered with Ryan.

"Why, Sara Hawkins," Elizabeth drawled in her deepest southern accent, "Ah do believe you've turned over a new leaf."

Sara detached herself from under Elizabeth's protective wing and moved to her front door. Winking boldly, she quipped, "Fig leaf."

Closing the door, she could hear Elizabeth still laughing at the old joke. Both Elizabeth and Ryan were being punny today. Although people ridiculed punsters, Sara appreciated the intelligence behind the witty twisting of words. *Nothing like being true to your own philosophy,* Sara mused as she strode into the bedroom and began changing clothes. Any whopper, prank, or

167

trick resulting in laughter was worthy of consideration.

She hugged herself. Love and laughter, she ruminated. Two of the best things in life were free. Food cost money, she added, patting "the cutest tush in town."

Humming a perky tune to match her mood, she pulled a pair of freshly pressed jeans out of the closet and put them on in the usual manner. She unsnapped her bra and flung it from the bed to a nearby chair, then chose a navy blue tank top out of the dresser and tugged it on over her head.

The hot dog and bean casserole had had the finishing touches put on it when she heard the doorbell ring.

"It's unlocked. Come on in," she shouted from the kitchen. Unable to resist a slice of hot dog covered with catsup, molasses, and bits of onion, she fished the piece out with her fingers and licked the sauce off before popping it into her mouth. "Hmmmm-hmmmm."

"My exact thought," Ryan said from the doorway. "May I have a taste?"

Sara reached for a dish towel to wipe her fingers with one hand and into the silverware drawer with the other. Ryan stopped her from completing either task. He raised her sticky thumb and forefinger to his lips.

"Hmmmm-hmmmm," he said, slowly licking any trace of brownish red sauce from her fingertips.

"That's very sexy." Sara gasped, feeling shivers run from the point of moist contact to the center of her nervous system, then catapult to each nerve ending.

He sucked the pad of flesh on her thumb as he pulled her close by wrapping his arm around her waist. "Now for the final taste test," he murmured, draping her arm over his shoulder.

The tip of his tongue traced the bow of her lower lip. "None there," he commented, his voice filled with teasing humor.

She nipped his tongue with her teeth. "Far be it from me to deny you anything." Her lips parted, she raised herself toward him with her arms around his neck until her toes dangled off the floor.

The low groan she heard from the back of his throat, his lips smiling at their own private joke of his inability to lift her as they kissed were better than any words complimenting her culinary skills. Ryan leisurely flicked the tip of his tongue on the delicate lining before probing, swirling, thrusting into the hot interior. The hint of sauce dissipated, replaced by the savory flavor of Ryan.

Their bodies strained against each other, and Sara's keen yearning surpassed any other experience. Ryan might be several inches taller, but he wasn't her superior any more than she was his. His caring matched her own. Man enough to see his misinterpretations, he forgave her shortcoming of jumping to conclusions. They were equal, craving oneness.

"Ryan," she whispered, tongue-tied, unable to express how she felt.

The smile she had encouraged, had learned to love curled the corners of his lips up. The lines of tiredness and stress seemed to have disappeared. Inch by inch he lowered her until her toes touched the tiled floor. His hands cupped her breasts.

"You take my self-control and leave me breathless," he said in an untypically hoarse voice. "You're missing something, aren't you?"

Sara shrugged, making her breasts bobble in his palms. "When I'm home, I don't bother with the modern version of a corset. Do you object?"

The gleam in his eye told her he didn't mind in the least. His thumbs buffed over the tips, making them turgid.

"Hmmm-hmmm." His dark eyes closed as though remembering them without the fabric covering. "They taste better than—"

"Wienies and beans?" Sara interjected, chuckling.

Ryan raised one eyelid. "You're incorrigible."

"That's better than being an embezzler," Sara said teasingly as she took two steps back and caught his hand between hers. She led him into the living room to the sofa. She curled into one corner, and he laid his head in her lap.

A bubble of laughter spilled from Ryan. "You set me up. The crown jewels thief, huh?"

"I thought you wanted proof I was worthy of being your accomplice," she sassily replied.

"And instead, I was asking subtle questions so

170

I could help you if you were in trouble." He shook his head at the understandable mixup. "After you had shattered my eardrum and refused to answer the phone, I considered storming the citadel."

Sara idly twirled a lock of the longish dark hair on the crown of his head. Her concentration divided itself between listening to Ryan and relishing the smooth silkiness between her fingers.

"Your legion of troops being the local police force? Brandishing a search warrant?"

"Not subtle enough." He winced at the playful tug. "The view from here is delightful."

He nuzzled the shadowed cleavage and inhaled deeply. *Lilacs,* he mused.

"What did you do?"

A half grin plastered on his face, he didn't answer for a moment, content with hooking his finger beneath her narrow shoulder strap and moving it to the side. With the same long finger he drew a line from her rounded chin, down her vulnerable sensitive neck, to the boundary made by the top.

"First I took a cold shower"—he paused, allowing time for her giggle—"to remove the salad, gumbo, water, and wine." Appearing to be anxious, he turned his head to scan the end tables and coffee table. "Since we're talking about embezzling, I wanted to make certain we don't destroy your place the way you did mine."

"Don't expect an apology from me. You maligned my character. Had you been able to get into my apartment after I had accused you,

171

what would have happened?" She didn't give him time to respond. She bent and gave him a hard, swift kiss. "You'd have smashed everything you could get your hands on."

"My intentions were honorable," Ryan said in self-defense. "I would have helped you."

"Uh-huh. Right into a wide-striped suit," she replied with a grin.

"Unfair accusation. From the beginning I could believe you were guilty. When a magnitude of evidence pointed in your direction, I decided to try to convince you to give up your wicked ways and let me help you."

"By seducing me?" Her blond eyebrow arching, her voice rising, she indicated her mocking disbelief.

"The seduction scene was your idea. Remember?"

"Are you complaining?"

"Remembering last night what took place in the master cabin of the sailboat is what caused the second cold shower, and the third, and the fourth." He punctuated each number with a string of kisses from one shoulder strap to the other. "You made sleeping impossible in my own bedroom, so I ended up stretched out on the back deck, watching the stars, and considered drowning myself for being such an ass."

"Poor darling," Sara cooed sympathetically while secretly eating up every word he said.

The buzzer ringing on the stove caught their attention. Sara swooped down to get one more kiss, then pushed him off her lap. She chuckled at the disappointed expression on his face.

"I've lost seven pounds since tangling with you. Tonight we build up our strength for"—she winked seductively—"investigating the ledgers at the bank." With a saucy twitch of her hips she walked into the kitchen, removed the casserole, and set it on the table. "The knives and forks are in the drawer by the sink. The glasses are in the cabinet above it."

"You have lots of dishes," he commented, tongue in cheek. "I don't suppose you'd consider donating them to a man who had a two-place setting completely destroyed by an act of vengeance, would you?"

Sara plunked herself down in the chair he held out for her. "They're part of my hope chest," she said in a broad hint. Actually they had been bought one at a time with each five-dollar purchase at the grocery store. But surely he didn't expect to pass the evening without a single windy story passing through her lips. "The dishes go with the owner."

"Subtle, Sara," he commented, wondering if she would propose uniting their stacks of dishes.

Her lips pouting provocatively, hiding the hint of an impish grin, she quipped, "You can eat off them, but this isn't a takeout joint."

Ryan laughed. Fork in hand, poised over the casserole she had dished out, he said soberly, "You never did tell me who the real thief is."

"No, I didn't," she answered tantalizingly, serving herself and starting to eat.

173

"Well?"

"Well, what?" Her innocent blue eyes fluttering, she extended the torture. "Oh! The embezzler."

He watched the twinkle in her eyes brighten as she began eating. *Pint-size devil,* he thought, loving the way her hand reached over and patted his leg in a comforting gesture.

"Right after dinner we'll go to the bank," he informed her. The way her finger drew lazy circles on his leg, matching the pace of her chewing, he knew her expectations were following another direction.

Her eyes narrowing, she nodded in agreement. She wasn't about to be accused of practicing her feminine wiles on him. Nor did she want his mind straying to the People's Bank at an inopportune moment.

But she could drive him crazy by touching him, she thought, amused. By the time they arrived at the bank he'd be drooling to get back to the condo. Her fingers walked up the sharp crease of his slacks, while she appeared to focus her attention on feeding herself.

Three-quarters of an hour later Ryan unlocked the bank doors after having explained to the night watchman their intention of working for a while. Sara let the tips of her unbound breasts rake across Ryan's arm as he held the door open.

His knees had threatened to buckle from the torturous caresses in the car. And now this. Every hair on his arm stood straight on end, then bent in her direction. He felt like a man who had condemned himself with his own smart mouth. *Sara, love,* he silently warned, *when I get you home* . . . He couldn't complete the thought without his imagination taking control of what little good sense that remained.

"This way," Sara crooned in a sultry touch-me-here voice. Her hips swaying, she sashayed toward her cage and deliberately paused. "I feel a whopper coming on," she said, covering her mouth.

"Stick strictly to the truth," he ground out between clenched teeth.

"Okay," she said grumpily. "You're drying up my creative juices, but I'll get the ledger out of Richard's cage."

"Richard Grant's cage? You're supposed to be responsible for returned Impact cards."

"I delegated the responsibility the way any effective supervisor would," she answered defensively. "I could hardly look him in the face today."

The tellers' cages were built for one person, not two. Ryan squeezed in beside her.

"Cozy, huh?" she asked as she rubbed against his zipper.

"Sara, my self-control is in shreds. So help me, I'll rip your clothes off and—"

"Some way for a vice-president to talk to the head teller," she interjected before he could finish his threat.

She opened the ledger to the place where a piece of paper stuck out. Her eyes widening, she gasped. "Oh, Jeez. He knew I knew. Listen to this." She began reading the neatly penned note with her name on top:

Sara:

I've had trouble facing you for months. Your furtive, bewildered looks today told me I'd been caught with my fingers in the till. There are no excuses for what I did, but I want you to know the reason.

Years ago I was married and fathered a child. About six months ago my teen-age daughter, higher than a kite on drugs, arrived on my doorstep. For a couple of months I tried to cure her problem with love. But an undemonstrative man by nature, I failed. I heard of a private hospital that helped teen-age addicts and placed her there. Too expensive, but necessary. My savings account didn't last long. Desperate, I devised a way to "borrow" money and return it before the customer became aware of the transactions. Since you're reading the Impact lost card ledger, you know exactly how I did it. It doesn't make me any less a thief, but every penny has been returned.

Much as I deplore the thought of disappointing you, of losing my job, of being humiliated publicly, the saddest part is . . . I'd do the same thing again to save my daughter.

Richard Grant

By the time she reached the bottom of the page, her voice had become husky and choked, and giant tears had formed in the corners of her eyes. "Poor, poor Richard."

She noticed the splotch on the paper made by one of her tears trickling down and landing on the paper. There were other similar splotches. Mentally she pictured Richard bending over the counter, carefully penning the note, tears streaking down his wrinkled face.

"Let me see the ledger," Ryan said, his own voice husky with emotion. Quickly he scanned the columns. "I don't see anything out of order."

"Good." Sara snuffled.

"He must have manipulated the date the card came in and the date the customer picked it up," he said, unable to detect any visible erasures. "What do you mean, good?"

"Ryan, don't you feel sorry for him?"

"Of course, but that doesn't excuse what he did."

"The money is back in the customers' accounts. As thorough as Richard is, they probably won't even know it was used for a good cause." Sara reached over the partition and grabbed a disposable tissue. She swiped it across one flooding eye, then the other. The tears refused to stop flowing. "You can't seriously be considering ratting on him. We could destroy the confession, so he knows I've read it, and say nothing to anybody else."

Ryan picked up the note, quickly folded it, and stuck it in his pocket. "Be sensible. The man knows how to siphon funds illegally. It may have been for tear-jerking reasons for the first time, but what happens when he runs a little short at the end of the month? Time to 'borrow' money again?"

"He won't. I know he won't. I'll do the

177

ledger." Sara leaned back in the cage to get as far away from Ryan as possible. The stubborn lifting of his chin silently refused her offer. "Where's your heart? You can't ruin a man's life because he helped his daughter!"

He slammed the ledger shut, grabbed one of her hands, and towed her out of the cage. "Dammit, you're putting business on a personal level."

Sara balked, digging her rubber-soled heels against the terrazzo-tiled floor to slow down his fast pace. "What the hell is a business made up of? People. People who care about each other. Who are willing to forgive temporary slips from right to wrong. Richard Grant is basically a good man."

"I'll do the best I can for him when I talk to Smith," he said.

Wrenching her wrist from between his fingers, she gasped. "You're going to the president of the bank?"

"Hell, yes!" he shouted. "We're both accomplices to the crime if we don't."

"Don't expect me to be a—"

Ryan grabbed her shoulders and slammed his mouth against the derogatory term he didn't want to hear. Once they had started hurling names at each other, there would be no turning back.

"I love you, Sara," he mumbled against her lips. "I promise. I'll do everything within my power to help him."

178

"Good. Let's burn the note before we leave the bank."

A heavy sigh passed through his teeth. "No."

"Oh, God, Ryan, don't do this to us." She pressed herself closer. Her arms wrapped around his waist, and she hugged him tightly. "Hold me. Let me feel your heart against my ear. Please, please," she begged.

For long, silent minutes they stood, locked together, swaying back and forth, clinging to their opposite beliefs of what was right and what was wrong.

"Let's go home," Ryan suggested. "Let's forget about the People's Bank, Richard Grant, and anything else that stands between us."

Sara scanned his dark features, hoping to see him relent. But the tenderness she saw in his eyes was for her, not for Richard Grant. She nodded and broke the embrace.

Not a single word was spoken on the way back to her condo. Each of them brooded over what had taken place, what would take place the next day.

Once inside the door, Sara whispered, "Will you stay with me tonight?"

"I don't think I could make it back to my place without you," he confessed. "But you can't use sex to change my decision."

Her blue eyes clouding, she bit her lip to keep from begging him again to change his mind. "You've come a long way from being No-Sense-of-Humor Crosby. You care about me. I only

179

wish you'd had time to learn to care about others."

"One step at a time," he whispered, taking single, slow steps toward her. "Meet me halfway."

Sara did more than meet him halfway. Generous by nature, she picked up his hand, which hung limply at his side, and led him to the bedroom. They undressed each other impatiently. By tormenting Ryan with glancing touches throughout dinner, on the way to the bank, in the bank, Sara had tormented herself equally. She wanted him. She needed him. She loved him and told him.

They were both right, both wrong, equally caught in the quagmire of their beliefs, their values. Throughout the night Ryan took, Sara gave, Sara took, Ryan gave. But in the grayness of the dawning light, holding each other in an intimate, tight embrace, they both feared separation.

CHAPTER TEN

With apprehension in her eyes Sara Hawkins watched Ryan enter the plush office of R. J. Smith, president of the People's Bank, Bay Branch. Deep in her heart there wasn't any doubt that Richard Grant would be jobless and in jail by noon.

Grant knew it, too. The expression on his face resembled that of a man who is next in line at the hangman's platform. His fate lay in the hands of two hard-shelled businessmen, who, Sara felt, considered the corporation more important than the people who performed the daily tasks to keep the business running smoothly.

She couldn't watch. One foot on the rung of her chair, the other on top of the burglar alarm, her head tilted to see over the counter, Sara restrained herself from rushing to the front office and pleading Grant's case.

"Pointless," she mumbled to herself. They weren't going to listen to softhearted, softheaded Sara.

Climbing down, she shivered. The cool air from the air-conditioning vent seemed to be directed straight at her spine. Her head jerked up when she heard Grant call her name. His arms folded on top of the partition separating their cages, he looked whipped.

"Don't take it badly, Sara. I knew the risks. I knew the consequences," he whispered in a quavery voice.

"Why didn't you borrow the money from the loan officer?"

"I'm at the top of my credit limit. My house is for sale and has been for months. I've borrowed on it extensively. The bank would never lend me another dime." He shrugged with futility.

"Dammit, Richard, I would have lent you the money," she said.

"Sweet, sweet Sara." He shook his head regretfully. "How could I have asked you to do that? But I do appreciate the offer."

Sara resisted the urge to reach up and pat his freckled hand. The tears she didn't want him to see were streaming down the back of her throat, making her gulp and choke.

"It's going to be embarrassing to have them take me out in handcuffs." Richard was musing aloud. "I hope the lobby isn't packed with customers."

He wasn't going out handcuffed, Sara vowed silently. "What are they doing now?" She didn't have the heart to climb back up on her perch to observe what was taking place.

"Smith and Crosby are hunched over the ledger book. Do they have the note?"

Sara bobbed her head up and down. "Ryan was with me when I checked the ledger. Before I could destroy the note, he pocketed it."

"Good for Ryan. I wouldn't want to have the burden of knowing I made you an accomplice. He did the right thing."

"What do you mean? He's in there snitching on you, and you say he did the right thing?" Her vision blurred when her eyes opened, and unchecked tears slid down her round cheeks.

"I'm the one who broke the rules. Don't blame him for my mistakes. He's right; I'm wrong." He handed Sara a tissue. "Why don't you go to the ladies' room and put some cold water on your face? I'll cover the windows."

"I don't want a gold watch," she muttered apologetically. "I'd rather have you."

Through her tears she saw the perplexed look on Richard's face. "Gold watch?"

"You know. The one they'll give me as a reward for catching—" The wry smile on his face stopped her flow of words. She mopped at her face.

"You're a charming lady who deserves a basketful of watches. Haven't you noticed the customers lining up at your window while the rest of us sit around doing nothing? Working next to you has kept me laughing rather than crying."

Sara sniffed. "My behavior is shocking. You've told me so a million times," she said, protesting the compliment. "Your drawer is neat and tidy;

mine is a disaster area. You're circumspect, the way a bank teller should be while I'm—"

"Delightfully amusing? Capricious?" Unexpectedly Richard chuckled. "Your sunny disposition even got to Crosby, didn't it?"

She couldn't answer, uncertain anyone could get to Ryan.

"Don't let this come between the two of you. He may not realize it, but he needs your bubbling personality more than any man I've ever met. When the rumor spread around the bank about his fiancée's jilting him . . ." Richard shook his head as though grieved.

"You knew? Everybody knew but me?"

"We also knew you had a Texas-size crush on him. I think it's wonderful you have finally gotten together. Sara, don't let what I did stand between the two of you."

A fresh well of tears built up behind her eyelids. She blew her nose with a decidedly unladylike honk.

"Go on to the ladies' room, Sara," he told her kindly.

After spinning around, Sara woefully trudged to the back of the bank, where the employee bathrooms were located.

Life wasn't fair, she silently wailed. Why did a nice, conscientious man like Richard Grant have to go to prison for helping his daughter? Dammit! What was money for if it wasn't to help the people you love? None of the customers had been hurt. He had paid the money back, for heaven's sake.

What did they want? A quart of blood? Poor Richard wasn't a young man. Didn't they realize he could die in prison? Her imagination took flight. She could visualize in black and white the funeral services. All the tellers would be at one end of the coffin, and Ryan and Mr. Smith would be at the other end. She could hear the prison chaplain's voice droning out a eulogy: "Richard Grant was a good man. But he made a mistake. Now he's paid for it."

"No!" Sara gasped in horror as she bent over the sink and splashed water on her face.

The fringe of blond, curly hair surrounding her face dripped water onto the front of her double-breasted fawn-colored summer suit. She didn't care. In the mirror she saw the red splotches on her cheeks, the pinkish rims around her eyes, the smudged mascara. She didn't care. How important was her appearance when poor Richard Grant had just been lowered into the ground? It wasn't.

"Sara! Sara, come quick."

The water dribbling off her chin splashed on the wall as she whipped her head around. "What's wrong?"

Ryan's secretary, Nancy Colston, grabbed her elbow and began dragging her toward the door. "Something's going on. Mr. Smith had me take a note to Richard. When Richard read it, he blanched, then shuffled toward Mr. Smith's office. Do you know what's happening?"

Sara tottered on her three-inch heels. Suddenly her knees and ankles felt weak, unable to support her ample frame. In a rush she stumbled out of the rest room and headed back to her cage. She had to see for herself.

Once inside her cage, she climbed up on her burglar alarm-chair rung perch. The three men sat in the president's office, grim expressions on their faces.

"What's going on?" Nancy asked, unable to see around Sara's body.

"Ryan is talking, pointing to Grant. R.J. is reaching for the phone."

Her left knee buckled. Sara clung to the top of the counter until she managed to get it back on top of the burglar alarm.

"Don't break an ankle!"

Sara felt hands on her waist helping her recover her balance. She kicked her shoe off. "Oh-oh. Who do you think he's calling?"

Glancing over her shoulder, she saw the doomed expression, heard the quick intake of air, then saw tears forming in the secretary's eyes. "The police?"

"Poor Richard. He doesn't want to be handcuffed and taken out of here. Do you think—" Her head snapped around, her eyes shifting from between the two doorways leading outside.

Four blue-uniformed men were rushing from the parking lot toward the doors, pistols drawn.

"Oh, no, they don't!" Sara exclaimed, kicking off her other shoe as she clamored down and ran lickety-split toward the front offices.

186

By the time she flung open the door to Smith's office the police were inside the front doors.

"No!" Sara shouted at Ryan. "He didn't do it. You can't let him die! I confess; I did it. *I took the money!"*

Ryan had jumped to his feet the moment she began shouting and started toward her, tempted to clamp his hand over her mouth. From the corner of his eye he saw the policemen enter the bank, guns out of their holsters.

"The bank is being robbed!" he announced, rushing out of the office as he dug in his pockets for the keys to the door. "Get down, everybody. Hit the floor."

Sara felt herself knocked to the carpet by the president of the bank. Richard rushed out, uncaring of the danger, willing to help Ryan.

Gasping to get some air back in her lungs, she struggled to get loose. "Let go!" she choked out. "Let go of me!"

"Stay still. The police are here. Ryan and Richard don't need you out there being shot at," R.J. muttered close to her ear.

"Shot at!" Sara sputtered, finally getting some air. She kicked her nylon-clad feet at the shins of the man holding her. "Let me up, dammit!"

Ryan was out there with bank robbers. He might be killed. The arm around her shoulder tightened the more she struggled. She had to get up, to help.

Ducking her head, she sank her teeth into the arm restraining her. She heard a grunt of pain near her ear. Instantly the one arm loosened, but the one around her waist tightened.

"Quit kicking and biting, Sara." R.J. flung his thigh over her pumping legs. "You'd just be in the way."

"You can get up," Richard informed them as he helped first Sara, then the bank president to their feet.

"What happened?" R.J. demanded, rubbing the teeth marks on his forearm as he charged toward the office door.

Ryan blocked his way. "Someone set off the burglar alarm in one of the tellers' cages."

Silence spread through the room like a thick layer of fog from the Gulf. The eyes of three men swung in Sara's direction simultaneously.

"Don't look at me. I didn't do it," she protested. "I mean . . . I took the money, but I didn't call the police."

"Sara, don't lie to cover for me," Richard interjected. He stepped past R.J. and moved toward her. "I've told them everything."

"He lied. Jeez, you can't let him die!" Sara wailed. "I'm young. Take me instead." She held her arms straight out, her wrists together as though waiting for the handcuffs.

"Let's all calm down," R.J. declared in a loud, authoritative voice. "We have embezzling, bank robbing, alarm setting, assault with a deadly weapon, and people dying, spinning around here like a beehive. Sit! All of you."

"But . . ." Sara began to object.

"Young lady," R.J. shouted, pointing to a vacant chair in front of his desk, "plant your butt in that chair. One more bite out of you, and I'll call the police myself."

"You bit the boss?" Richard asked. He covered his mouth to keep a chuckle from bursting out.

"Sorry." Remembering protocol, Sara added, "Sir."

Ryan moved to stand behind the chair she sat down in. Richard sank into the chair beside her.

"Now." R.J. continued to rub his arm as he eased himself into his chair behind the desk. After picking up a gold-toned pen, he quickly jotted down a list. His gray eyebrows rising over pale blue eyes, he stated, "First on the agenda: embezzling. Richard confessed first. Sara confessed loudest."

"Richard lied to protect me," Sara quickly volunteered. "Don't listen to anything he says—"

"Sara, shut up," Ryan suggested in a mild tone. "We may have to gag her."

R.J. grinned and nodded his head. "Her tongue is as sharp as her teeth and heels. Be careful."

Glancing up, Sara glared at Ryan. *Nobody is going to muzzle me,* she communicated to him with flashing blue eyes.

"My written confession is on your desk," Richard insisted, having regained his composure.

Sara immediately refuted him. "I'll put mine in writing," she said.

The president of the bank shook his head and raised his eyes heavenward as though seeking divine guidance. "I've talked to the bank's attor-

189

ney. I'm certain that since restitution has been made, we'll be able to work something mutually agreeable out with Richard. Does that curb your creative writing urges, Sara?"

"You mean you won't prosecute? He won't go to prison?" Sara asked, leaning toward the man in authority and away from Ryan. She watched the bank president nod his head solemnly.

"Ryan has gone to bat for Richard." A look passed between the two men. Then R.J. leveled his eyes on Sara. A grin lurked at the corners of his mouth. "I'm not certain he'd do the same for you. He's partial to ties that reach his tie tack."

Sara covered her eyes with both hands and audibly groaned. The three men chuckled at her gesture.

"I'll take full responsibility for my future wife's actions," Ryan stated, his voice coated with laughter.

Her hands dropping from her face, Sara's head twisted up. "Future wife?" she muttered in disbelief.

"We'll put that at the bottom of the agenda," R.J. said, scribbling on the list. "Next is bank robbing and burglar alarm setting."

Ryan cleared his throat. "The red switch is flipped up to the activated level in the head teller's cage."

"Ooooops," Sara mumbled. "I can explain."

"Please do," R.J. said. "Try to stick as close to the truth as you can. Knowing you, I'll hear some wild tale about elephants herding themselves through the bank."

190

"No elephants, sir. I'm too short to see over the cage, so I put one foot on the rung of the chair and my knee on top of the alarm. My foot slipped," she explained truthfully.

"Ryan, requisition a small footstool for her to stand on. So much for robbers and alarms. Assault with a deadly weapon," he read, checking off the items as he went along. "Sara apologized for kicking my shins and biting my arm. Should I prosecute or not, gentlemen?"

"She really shouldn't bite the hand that feeds us," Ryan said, struggling to keep the laughter out of his voice.

"It's your fault. Rushing out there where you could be killed," Sara said.

"My wife blames me for everything, too," R.J. commented, chuckling out loud. "After thirty years it gets to be an endearing trait."

"I'll accept the blame." Ryan chuckled. "I'm trying to figure out how I'm going to accept responsibility for the last item. Sara, who's dying?"

"You're the most likely candidate if you keep laughing," she said, smiling at him cheekily.

"Which brings us to the last item on the list: a wedding. Well?" R.J. glanced from Sara to Ryan and back again. "Why don't the two of you take the afternoon off and discuss this privately? I'll expect to be asked to be one of the witnesses who sign the bottom of the marriage license." Grinning broadly, he looked at Sara and added, "Otherwise, I might not believe it."

"Me either," Sara muttered, uncertain whether or not Ryan meant the public proposal.

Ryan took her hand, laced his fingers through hers, and helped her out of the chair. "We'll get your purse, then leave."

Sara propped her other hand on R.J.'s desk and leaned forward. "He's always making me pay for lunch," she whispered confidentially. "Now that he's going to be a married man, supporting eight or ten kids, do you think he could get a raise?"

"Sara!" Ryan groaned, propelling her toward the door.

She could hear R.J. and Richard laughing boisterously as Ryan possessively dragged her out the front door. Waving jauntily, she messaged silent kisses back to the employees and customers, who grinned at them.

Outside, she jumped up and flung her arms around his neck. "Did you mean it?"

Ryan grinned her favorite lopsided grin. "Remember your suggesting the only time I smiled is when you kissed me? Well, I've decided the only way to keep you from telling windy stories is the same remedy."

His smiling lips closed over the teeny gasp coming from between her awaiting parted lips. *Laughter and love* hummed merrily in her mind, *love and laughter . . . and happily ever after.*